Back, Belly, & Side

True Lies and False Tales

Conversation Pieces

A Small Paperback Series from Aqueduct Press
Subscriptions available: www.aqueductpress.com

About the Aqueduct Press
Conversation Pieces Series

The feminist engaged with sf is passionately interested in challenging the way things are, passionately determined to understand how everything works. It is my constant sense of our feminist-sf present as a grand conversation that enables me to trace its existence into the past and from there see its trajectory extending into our future. A genealogy for feminist sf would not constitute a chart depicting direct lineages but would offer us an ever-shifting, fluid mosaic, the individual tiles of which we will probably only ever partially access. What could be more in the spirit of feminist sf than to conceptualize a genealogy that explicitly manifests our own communities across not only space but also time?

Aqueduct's small paperback series, Conversation Pieces, aims to both document and facilitate the "grand conversation." The Conversation Pieces series presents a wide variety of texts, including short fiction (which may not always be sf and may not necessarily even be feminist), essays, speeches, manifestoes, poetry, interviews, correspondence, and group discussions. Many of the texts are reprinted material, but some are new. The grand conversation reaches at least as far back as Mary Shelley and extends, in our speculations and visions, into the continually-created future. In Jonathan Goldberg's words, "To look forward to the history that will be, one must look at and retell the history that has been told." And that is what Conversation Pieces is all about.

L. Timmel Duchamp

Jonathan Goldberg, "The History That Will Be" in Louise
Fradenburg and Carla Freccero, eds., *Premodern Sexualities* (New
York and London: Routledge, 1996)

Published by Aqueduct Press
PO Box 95787
Seattle, WA 98145-2787
www.aqueductpress.com

10 9 8 7 6 5 4 3 2 1
ISBN: 978-1-61976-081-3

The following stories were previously published:

"Name Calling," *Abyss and Apex*, Feature Story, May 2014

"Jumbie from Bordeaux," *Margin's Magical Realism*, Spring/Summer
2004; *Calabash*, Fall/Spring 2004

"Single Entry," *Moko Magazine*, First Issue, November 2013; *Genesis: An Anthology of Black Science Fiction*, 2010

"The Dreamprice," *The Caribbean Writer*, Volume 7, 1993

"Responding in Kind," *Calabash*, Fall Spring 2004

"Now I Got Girl," *Scarab*, edited by Sheree Renee Thomas, 2006

Cover illustration courtesy Richard Baker

Original Block Print of Mary Shelley by Justin Kempton:
www.writersmugs.com

Printed in the USA by Applied Digital Imaging

Conversation Pieces
Volume 45

Back, Belly, & Side

True Lies and False Tales

by
Celeste Rita Baker

To all my loved ones who were, are and will be again. Thanks for spending this lifetime with me. Thanks for pushing, guiding, and uplifting me.
And thank you for welcoming me into this wonderful Circle.

Contents

Single Entry

Carnival time come, and I a single entry. I not in any troup or nothing. I just parading in me costume, all by meself. Everybody asking me what song dat is and where me music coming from. I tell dem I write de song, which is true, and it coming from a iPod and dese liddle speakers ringing me North and South Poles, which not true. I projecting de song from me core, but dey ain't need to know dat.

De sun hot, just like I like it, and no clouds dressing de sky. De crowds of people is like from before, when people didn't used ta be 'fraid of crowds. All de children dem being told ta keep still, but dey can't, from de excitement in de air. Grown folks drinking all kinda rum and eating with dey fingers. Water and ice giving way for free ta keep people from passing out in de heat. De music blasting, bumping, blaring so as ta make de ground shake. Heart and hips can't help but keep de beat, de groove growing to encompass all a dem like wet cover water.

It start ta happen when I finish in Post Office Square. Dat's de big demonstration place. You balance you high wid you sober and do you best dance dere. Try ta remember you routine if you have one. Impress de judges and give people a good show. Make de camera dem like you so de people at home could feel like dey dere bam-boushaying wid you.

Before Post Office Square is de start of Main Street where it have de old warehouses, which make inta expensive stores lining both sides of de narrow street. It hard for some of de bands and costumes to pass through cause it so narrow. But I like it cause it intensify de sounds and all de colors feel like hot pepper in you eye, so bright. But den when you pass out inta de Square de vibes change, because it so big, like swimming from a river inta de clean blue sea. I blow up me presence ta fill de whole Square.

Single entry me 'rass. I was everybody and everything. I was de whole friggin' planet. De globe I telling you, de world dancing on two feet. Course you couldn't self see me feet. And I no touch de ground.

On Main Street de people push back, push back ta make me pass. Everyone grinding pon one anodda. Is smiles, cheers, and waves. De children hush quiet wid awe, de grown folks rushing me, trying ta touch, ta see if me water wet. Try find de string between de sun and me. De moon and me. Try see how a cloud what seem ta be above Cruz could have de frangipani trees dem dripping in old Tutu. How I bright where de sun reach and dark when I turn 'round. You like it, eh?

When I reach de Square is blow I blow up. Before I was 'round twenty-five feet at me equator, but I was fifty by de time I reach de Judges Stand. Ole Lady Stinking Toe petals drippin from me steada sweat. Jasmine petals drifting in me breeze scenting de whole Square. I have volcanos erupting on de bass and trade winds blowing loud like horns. Earthquakes trembling de drums. Is de earth song, you see. I's de earth. And dey loving me.

De crowd gone wild. Dey never see nothing so. De oceans sloshing and Rock City really rocking. Cameramen zooming in, capturing a single live guana sunning on Coral Bay. Let 'em look dey look. We all here, Everytreerockstoneandflea.

I could dance too, you know. And not only spin, neida, though me bounce ain't so high and does take quite a while. Every now and again I does let off some sparks in de air. Stars burning bright.

Dey loving me and I loving dem too. Feeling all de liddle souls tickling me, tickling me, and I glad.

When time ta move on I shrink down ta fit again. Less people here and dey more watching each odda dan me. I feeling little pains, like a drilling and a cutting and a breaking up. Shrinking faster dan I want, and I can't stop atall. Time I pass Joe's Bar I hardly de size of a big car. By Senior Citizen's Viewing Stand I coulda fit inta a black plastic garbage bag. On de way ta de Field de people dem clap and smile, but I could tell dey seen too much ta pay special mind ta me. Is de crowd energy dat let me blow up so. Make all me beautiful intricacies flow just so. Now only a few people studying me, and I dripping and losing form. Mud sliding and whales beaching. I turnoff and head back ta de parking lot ta go have a drink in de Village.

Wellsir, I can't self see de counter. I smaller dan a greedyman's dream and can't make no arms again neida.

People tripping over me, cussing, and is smaller and smaller I getting. Little boy try ta pick me up like I was a toy throw way in a gutter. I make thunder, he ain't hear. De most I could do is get up some lightening, and he drop me. I roll under a table and hunch up next to a leg.

Parade done. Sun gone down. People streaming inta de Village for Last Lap. Last drink, last dance, last chance

3

ta have big fun. Everybody in a frenzy ta get and ta have. Nobody ain't see me. I hear dem talking 'bout me, dat single entry. So pretty. So magical. So sure ta win. And I deydey, kick under de bar. Huddling in de dark, rum and hot grease dripping down through me mountains.

Now I Got Girl

Fitting into the costume wasn't hard. Making myself believe I looked sexy as a construction paper and felt sunflower was hard.

Sunshine and flowers ain't my thing. I prefer mood lighting. Strobe lights look good in my hair. My natural setting is behind a bar where I get to use my fast hands and slow smile. I'd rather have bad sex in the back of a raggedy Corolla than get out of bed before three.

But I was doing it for Girl, of course.

I got Girl like this.

About a year ago I was strolling home. The moon was practically at eye level, so I knew it was about ten after four, teetering just a little in my blue leather thigh highs with the seven-inch heels. Mind in the gutter, head in the clouds. And there she was, right in the middle of the sidewalk, like one of those orange danger cones. At first I thought she was a gargoyle. The man I'd just left looked a little like a gargoyle himself, and with my head not right I thought this was his little gargoyle love child. She was so still she coulda been a statue that fell off a building and forgot to break. But her crying hit the kind of high notes that sent arrows straight through my eyeballs.

I looked around to see who was tending to this, but no one was paying her any mind. I'd just passed the regular block watchers, but they'd acted like they didn't see me. They'd been there all day and all night, so I knew they knew something. Maybe she pitched a fit and is crying it out. Can't have any more candy or whatever girls cry over. I'd just walk on by, minding my own business. I don't like children, the sneaky little beasts, so I kept an eye on her the way you would watch a rabid dog. Nice doggy. Stay back.

I gave her plenty of room. I was practically in the street. Then the little pit bull, and that's exactly what she looked like, with a wide fat face and ears set way up high on her head, springs up from the sidewalk like a splash from a puddle and clamps herself to my hips.

It ain't the first time my hips been clamped. I've had men who use their hands for a living clamp onto me and I can buck 'em off in two shakes, if I want to. But this little crumb-snatcher had a grip like a lug wrench. I tried to stomp her feet with my stilettos, but it wasn't easy. My teeny weeny purse came down on her head at least three, four times, but it only rebounded and hit me in the titties. I really didn't want to touch her at all, who knew what kind of chiggers she had? But I got one hand around the back of her skinny little neck and tried to yank her head off. All that did was force her snotty face off my white sequined hot pants, leaving a shiny string of spit from her lips to my hips.

"What's the matter with you?" I shrieked, "What the fuck you think you doing? Get offa me!"

She looked about four. Braid extensions hanging all down her back. Little orange halter top, pink shorts. Cheap green high-heeled sandals. Very inappropriate. Covered in goose bumps. Wailing like a banshee.

I looked back at the men on the corner. Men I'd just passed. Passed every night. Deadpan faces. Not seeing or hearing a thing.

"Hey, Looney!" I yelled, louder even than the little creature. "Looney, Spite, Michael! Get this thing offa me! Whose is this?"

They all looked at me. But that's all they did. Any other time they'da been all up in the happenin. They got my back. Normally. But this time they acting like I gotta handle the little street urchin by myself. Guess they thought it'd be no problem for me to drop kick the little animal. Or something.

I turned around and tried walking. I couldn't punt her away, her body center was too high and too close. Maybe a roundhouse would send her flying, but probably me too. I was determined to lose the little carpetbagger before I got to my building.

"I have to go to the bathroom," she said, clear as Bobby Blue Bland, then she started bellowing again, along the lines of James Brown.

"So? Go home," I screamed, kinda in the Patti LaBelle hysteria vein.

"I really have to go bad."

By this time I'm outta breath. Felt like I was fighting the devil's granddaughter. I turned the corner of my block, cutting it close to the filthy bricks, hoping to scrape her off, but she swung around my ass like a lasso twirling around a horse's neck.

"Where's your mother?" I asked. These things have mothers don't they? They ain't supposed to be walking around at the crack of dawn accosting people. "Where do you live?"

That's when she chose to shut up. Just whimpered and wiped her nasty face on my dry-clean-only pants. Threw her big head all the way back and looked up at me. Her jaw hung open like it was unhinged. Looked like a bird waiting on a worm.

Oh, God, I thought, suppose the little squirt's lost? All kindsa bad things happen to kids. I barely escaped myself. My grandfather raised me. Well sort of. He took me from my mother and I lived with him. We ate together and he smiled at me at least once a day, so that was okay. Mama's brain didn't sit right in her head, and there were plenty days and nights when I'd hear Grandpa chasing her from around our door. Some folks, be they kin or not, he'd said, just don't mean you no damn good whether they want to or not.

I should turn around and take her straight to the police, I thought.

And there they were. Squad car had rolled up on us quiet as a hearse. Little Bit slid behind me like a shadow, and I clean forgot that I coulda been glad to see them. We both froze, tryna be invisible until they were gone.

"OK. Now," I said, pulling myself together and snatching her around in front of me, "How'd you get here? Where're you supposed to be?"

Again she didn't answer, but she took a few of those shuddering deep breaths, and I knew she was gonna let loose with another set of bawling and all kindsa pain would knock me to my knees. So I did the only thing I could.

Flung myself against the wall of the building, too fast for the little brat. Knocked the wind right out of her.

I took a couple of steps.

"I really gotta go bad," she said, and almost pulled my pants off as she latched onto me again. "Oh, no, it's starting to come out!"

"You better not!" I screamed and tried to pry her off like a scab. "Pee in the street! What the fuck do I care?"

"I can't!" she screamed back, "I'm a lady!"

॰

She started doing the pee-pee dance in the elevator. Worked into the Watusi while I was unlocking my door and was damn near doing the Philly dog by the time I pointed down the hall. She went first.

She was quick. I'll say that for her. And didn't leave a mess. Had washed her hands and rinsed off the soap, and didn't use my towel.

When I came out the kid was standing in the hall looking around at my apartment. Which is nice, even if I say so myself. I got lots of plants and good windows and a "music is my life" stereo. I got a white rug too, which I'm glad she ain't standing on.

Not that she's dirty. I can see now that she ain't dirty. Even those long fake braids, which I think are too grown-up for little girls, not to mention bad for the ego, are fresh and neat. Child got on pink nail polish, I see, as one hand goes up to play with her ear and she shoves her other thumb in her mouth.

I went to the kitchen to get a drink and she followed me, those ridiculous plastic heels making more noise than mine.

Beer in hand I went back to the door and opened it wide.

"Out," I said, "Go back where you came from. Out! Out!"

She made a move like she was going, but it was just a feint cause she launched herself at me like a torpedo and we both fell to the floor. She was crying and I was cussing.

She didn't know who she was. Not really. Said her name was Chardonnay and her mother's name was Keisha. They used to live in a big building. Not around here. But her mother told her they didn't live there no more, and now she don't know where she live. Phone number was four six two. Last name? Alize. Chardonnay Alize. Uh-huh. Grandmother?

"You mean Annabelle?" she said. "Keisha mother? She don't like me. She don't like Keisha neitha."

"Of course she likes you."

"No she don't," she said, talking around her thumb. "She told me. Told Keisha she shoulda got rid of me. Told Keisha she don't care where we go, just get outta her face."

I had another beer to steel myself for calling the police. I didn't know what else to do. Lost and Found for people is the police, right? So that's who I had to call. I ain't done nothing wrong, what I got to be scared of? Still I was shaking so much I could hardly see the numbers on the stupid little phone. The girl was standing in front of me watching my every move. Her knees were buckling she was so tired. But I refused to tell her to sit down. When I got through to them they didn't give me a hard time, but they didn't give a damn either. Not that I cared, but they supposed to act like it. Said call Administration for Children's Services. They said they'd come and get her, but wouldn't say when. First they wanted to know all about me. What's my middle name? What's my social security number? Where did I work? What's my phone number? My cell phone number? Was I on welfare? Food stamps? Shit wasn't about me! They pissed me off. Child in trouble, they supposed to be on it. Faster than a speeding bullet.

I even called Animal Control. They came right away, but they wouldn't take her. I fell asleep with the phone in my hand. When I woke up Girl was curled up on my lap. I gotta take those damn braids out, I thought. Wait. What?

I, we, went looking for Looney right away. He told me that Keisha dropped Girl off a little before I got there. Said she stopped by, on her way to Greensboro she said, with some guy in a 1966 brown and cream V-8 Thunderbird. Told him Chardonnay was his daughter and he could have her. Looney said it could be true, but hell, this the first he heard of it. He patted her on the head like a puppy. I thought he was gon' scratch her behind the ears.

I, we, went back upstairs. I had rum in my coffee. She had scrambled eggs and milk.

Grandpa had put rum in his coffee when he was talking himself into something, or out of something. When he was finishing something or starting something. When he needed to make the bumpy smoothe. For me, for him, for anyone. He drank a lot of rum.

I take better care of my shoes than some people take of they children.

I ain't never had nothing this long. Now I do all kinds of unimaginable bullshit. I make no-lump Cream of Wheat at six a.m. when I should be just dozing off. We been to every children's museum and craft-making hoodoo bullshit in this city. I seen more storytellers and puppets than Corolla's, I'll tell you that. And all of them in the daytime. I already knew she could dance and suspected she could sing from the way she wailed that first night, but she's really good with numbers and math. She counts my tips while I make breakfast and understands some, more, less, and share, which other people call fractions, addition, subtraction, and division. She's learning to read too, not just words, but people, which I think is just as important so she doesn't get caught up in other people's mess.

I had to give up beer to buy a good birth certificate to prove the little leech existed. And clothes. Looney helps me with the clothes and such. Girl likes dresses. She the only little girl I know likes dresses. Says she wants to look like a lady so she'll be treated like a lady.

"Little girl lady," I remind her.

"Okay," she says "little girl lady, but still everybody gotta be nice to me."

"Uh-huh," I say.

I only cuss at work now, and I don't hit her at all. Anymore. I got Mrs. Bryan from 12B watching her while I work at the bar. She's the only one I trust.

I still can't stand the little Post-It. Got me all dressed up like a damn sunflower for a kindergarten play. Girl, of course, looks good in her bumble bee costume that I made her, with that big ole smile, while me, my petals are all droopy and my leaves look like I got worms. Next year I'll probably be a fire hydrant. By the time the little wart graduate from college I won't have no dignity at all.

Jumbie from Bordeaux

I was frighten from de time I wake up. I ain't trust
de way de sun creep over de top of de mountain, like
it sneaking. I ain't trust de way de chickens crowing. Instead of de sing song dat make me tink dey telling jokes,
I hear a squawking, kinda bawling, like ain't nothing
funny. I ain't want ta leave me bed.

But I get up and go outside, round de back. De chickens scatter like dey never see me before. I put me hand
over de coal pot and feel de heat. It have some dough
dere on de side, but it ain't fry. Where Mommy? Mommy
never leave a hot coal pot alone, where we children could
reach. Ain't I a child no more? I musta get grown in de
night, cause a child does get breakfast, piece of dumb-
bread, or johnny cake, and I ain't see none for me. I
strut off ta find everybody, hands in me pockets like a
big man. Plantation quiet quiet. Even though I don't like
ta get up, I like de morning cause de air smell like it
just bathe. We high up from de sea, but when de morning breeze blow it bring de sea smell. Sometimes I close
me eyes, when it blow liddle hard, and is like I feeling
de small waves push me 'round. Like when we had go
down ta de sea and Daddy hold me under he arm like a
soggy tree branch and tell me to lay out on de water like
is Mommy lap I laying on. See how nice he tell me, soft
and warm. Leave de water hold you up he say. And it did.

I was floating. I jump up to tell Mommy "Look!" and de float gone. Daddy laugh and grab me again. I float all day feeling de small waves rocking me.

Today not even liddle breeze blowing. De bad feeling come round again. Dis time a morning everybody be cutting cane already. I going try meet up with de wagon. Is my job ta tie up de cane in bundles. Big piles of cane lay down here and dere, and de wagon man Joseph and me, since I make me seventh birthday, travel up and down de field gathering dem. All day we go back and forth, hauling what Mommy, Daddy, and de odda grown folks cut, all de way to de clear yard by de Massa house near de front road. Is hard work, but de new Massa say I big enough to do it. De ole Massa die, and he wife and children all leave when de new Massa come. He come with evil ways Daddy say. But Mommy say hush, try not ta tink on dat. But I don't like looking at de new Massa, or Missus neida. Dey skin too paley paley, like dis de first dey ever see sun and he eyes had make me itch. De day he make us line up, de day he tell me I was big enough to bundle, was de first time I see him close up and he eyes almost clear, like lizard belly, and I tink on de dead lizard I see de day before, covered over wid black ants. I start ta scratch and rub, 'til Mommy pinch me, tell me be still. 'Til now he does make me itch when I see him.

I hear somebody crying. And somebody shushing dem. Coming from down by de clear yard. I don't want to go, but me feet take me. Is a long walk dat take only a short time.

I ain't look up. Just follow de dusty trail 'til I reach a circle of ragga skirt hems almost reaching de ground. Pant leg too. Some short, showing lot of scarred-up legs, some long, dragging in de back like foot have tails. I 'fraid to look now. What I had want to find, I ain't want to see.

Everybody standing tight tight together. Quiet.

Is not really hot, but I sweating. I start looking for me Mommy, me Daddy, pushing through de big people. Mommy woulda make me stop pushing and say 'scuse me, but I can't self find she yet. Everybody gather 'round de two tamarind trees. Dey stand big in de clear yard, and shade de house. Two a dem, so close together and so big, dat de high branches all tangle up. Me and Jacko and Maryann does climb to get de ripe tamarind when Massa not home.

When I done push me way near de front, me Auntie grab me and hold me tight 'gainst she back. Me chest push up on she barna. She two arms reaching back to hold me two arms.

"...don't care what you did before, but I'm your new master and there will be no more fornication! Do you understand me? No sex. No men and women laying together. No sleeping together. No sneaking around at night to get to one another. I've told you this before, and I will not tolerate disobedience!"

Me ain't know what Massa yelling about, but de grown folks ain't like it. Is like all a dem just turn to stone. I can't see nothing but Auntie dress back and I try turn me head. Nobody say "yes, Massa," nobody say "no, Massa." No breeze blow, nobody breathe.

"Now, this one...umh, Audra and this one, Louis, have been caught at...are known to be...when I want you to breed, goddammit, I will breed you!"

I don't know what all he say but Audra and Louis is me Mommy and Daddy. I know Mommy name is Audra, only Daddy does call she dat. 'Specially at night, so far night is almost morning, I does hear he calling she Audra 'steada Sal, what everybody else call Mommy. Dey does be talking and whispering and making loud soft sounds and dat's how I know dat Audra and Louis is Mommy and Daddy.

I getting more frighten now and I need to find dem bad bad. De sun hot on me head and I ain't know why Auntie holding me so tight. I can't self breathe and me legs feeling like jellyfish look. I jerk 'round hard and before Auntie could wrench me back, I see.

What I see make me head throw back and a scream fly out. So loud and so long I could feel it trembling de air 'round me. Dat too frighten me and I feel like candle wax, melting into de ground. Is like de sound alone make inta a ting and me insides ripping out.

Stretched out hard, flat on de ground, bare naked, is me *Mother*. And me *Father*. De Massa standing on one side, de headman on de odda. Dey gon' whip dem. De whips long long and brown. Three piece a leather braid up together, de bottom free like feathers. Long time dey hang on a hook by ole Massa door. De only time I ever see dem move from dere was when a slobbering, red-eyed dog had come in de yard and everybody chase him down. Ole Massa had grab de whip den and whoosh it through de air so fast you ain't sure you see it. It land on de dog back and bright red blood come out.

I see de whip handle in new Massa hand, raise up high over he head. Massa and headman watch each odda, like dey gon' race. De people quiet. 'Cept for me, I ain't stop screaming. Me Uncle, John Frank holding Massa gun.

"Shut that boy up," Massa say. He voice like dark cloud holding rain, and Uncle John Frank point Massa gun at Auntie and me. I see tears rolling down he face.

I still screaming when de first lash come down. Den me Mommy join me. She call de angels with she mouth, but dey ain't come. We two voices soaring through de morning like cutlass. Auntie try cover me mouth with she two hands. Daddy shaking like fish quiver when it come on land. De lashes falling on me parents bare skin.

De *helplessness* jump out a me and latch onta something dat *could*. Is like I fly right out me own mouth. Went wid me own scream and find meself high up in de air, swooping down from de sky like a stone from a slingshot.

I see de tops of de two tamarind trees and de half circle of people gather 'round. I see me Mommy and Daddy stake out on de ground like two pigs for roasting, dey brown bodies looking blurry in de brown dirt. Everybody still but Auntie. She turning 'round now, trying to hold me up, but me body fall right down to de ground, heavy like sleep.

Every time de two whips draw back dey smacking leaves off de trees. Leaves falling like sweat.

I rush at Massa first. I meaning ta take out he eye. Gouge out he throat. Snatch de whip from he hand like I does snatch worm from de dirt.

De whip nearly catch me when I dive in, but I reach he face and try plow me whole body in through he eye hole. He arm fly up and try bat me away. I feeling stuck in de mush of he eye and is like sucking mud to try get 'way. I use me feet to scrabble and claw. He screaming too now and de lash fall with no force.

I turn and fly at de headman. He watching me come, mouth hanging open, looking stupid. He gone catch more dan flies today.

Massa yelling, clutching he face, "Shoot it! Shoot it, John Frank! Shoot!"

17

Straight for de headman's face I go, me talons stretch out like I ready ta clutch a rat. He try raise he whip to me, but it too late, I grab hold of he two cheeks and try reverse meself and take he flesh wid me.

Uncle John Frank can't shoot. I too close. He swing de gun like a club, but I gone already and he bash in headman nose. I drop headman two cheek in de dirt and fly away.

Dey leave Mommy and Daddy tie up dere in de dirt.

Auntie had done take de body where I used ta be and lay it on de selfsame bed I ain't want ta get up from. She know I dead, and she crying.

Auntie go back and cut de ropes holding Mommy and Daddy down by sheself. Nobody else would come. She bring water for dem. Blood oozing every time dey draw breath. Dey eyes open but dey ain't really seeing. Can't stand up, can't sit down, de whole back a dem torn up. Auntie crying, not letting she tears fall on de deep deep cuts. De Missus in de window watching. And I dere, in de tamarind tree, watching she back.

Auntie bring a bowl a water for me too. She watch me wid she face turn sideways, but she call me by me name. "Come, Clem, drink," she say and is den I feel ta cry. She know me. Auntie know me. I ain't self know meself, bound up in feathers wid beak and ting, same bloody as de two whips drop down in de dirt.

I never sleep inna bed again.

Name Calling

Ah wake up every morning at thirteen minutes before three. Imagine. Every foreday morning, de same thing. Heart racing, palms sweating, singing out a name. Any and all kinda name. Jaramogi, Hanako, Melissa, Ansgar, William. Ah write dem down. Ah have several notebooks just full of de names. Dunno dese people, strangers all. Ain't but about three or four people I could call on dis, me island home of Tania, good times or bad. Yet Ah calling dese names with force and command, knowing, just knowing dat whatever is going on is for true and for sure.

Dis has been going on for two years and ten months. Only two things Ah could remember when Ah wake up, dat somebody had call me, call for me, and dat somebody name was Ramona or Franklin or Marshall or whosoever it was dat time, dat night. Ah answer dem with dey own name and it done. Me ain't ever hear de same name twice. Ah couldn't find nothing in no dream books, none of de of ole folks could tell me nothing. Ah ask de lottery ticket sellers and de Obeah women, de one who does only wear black and de one who only wear white. De two a dem cross dey chest and spit on de ground but dey say dey ain't heard about dat before. After dat Ah ain't talk about it again, in case people start talking melee about me. So without no answer Ah just write down de names and keep going. What else Ah gon' do?

But something happening now. Something changing. Ah still waking up. It's always two forty seven in de morning. But me ain't getting no name. And instead of feeling happy and rested, like Ah'm used to feeling, ever since Ah realize wasn't nothing going to come of me getting all worked up, instead of de refreshment Ah'm accustomed to, morning come and Ah'm suffering. Ah feel like Ah ain't turn off de stove when Ah done cook, ain't lock de door when Ah leave de house, ain't collect me pay when Ah finish work. Ah only getting half a night's sleep now, going on three months. First month people say, "hey, Rhonda, you lose weight, you lookin good." Now dey watch me like Ah have AIDS, and nobody don't get too close. Me hair brittle and falling out, and me eyes look like Ah packing for a cruise on one of de big ships dat dock at de harbor. Ah dragging through de days in de hotel making beds and swishing bathtubs, tips going down down since Ah can't find a smile to sell. Emanual don't come 'round no more, say Ah too grouchy. De children call from dey big lives in bigger places, but Ah rush dem off de phone. Inside Ah feel like somebody calling me all de time, bawling out me name, calling for me. Ah feel Ah always going to dem, answering dem, and Ah just too too busy.

Me best girlfriend, she name Erma, from when we was small together, back when de weather was hot and breezy, not heated and rainy like now, causing tourism to drop off and halve everyone's little piece of money, anyway she, she take me to her doctor. Say mine too modern minded, like is science alone dat rule de world. Is cash money Ah have to pay to see she doctor, since he don't take my insurance and he come telling me it's stress. Of course it's stress, but he ain't tell me what Ah could do about it more dan eat, exercise, sleep, and drink plenty water. How else he think I manage to stay on de planet fifty-nine years? Ah just suck me teeth and turn off.

Den Erma say she want us go to Antler's Bay next week, where it quiet and peaceful. Is a harassment Ah say. Long car ride, short ferry ride on de choppy sea, next long ride in a hot bus full of strangers. Tuesday, me next day off, she want to go. She had to take de day off. Ah know she worried about me. Ah ain't fight she. Ah say okay.

When time come to board de bus to de beach Erma take one look at me face, even though me ain't complaining, and she hire a taxi. De air conditioning hit me and it feel good. Ah close me eyes and just breathe. Ah feel Erma take me hand in hers own. Names, old names, names Ah had done already write down swirling 'round in me mind. Bolo, Gloria, Misha, Warren.

Taxi stop, and we ain't at Antler's Bay, but some cleared patch a land near a beach Ah don't recognize. When de heat of de day hit me Ah feel dizzy and think me belly calling to me besides. Erma lead me into a wood-board house paint up in red yellow blue and white star shapes. De paint so new it burning me eyeballs. Ah glad when we pass up de porch steps and de open counter bar to reach de insides. It make up like a restaurant, except ain't no customers. A man, scrawny as a mangy dog, come in from behind an old sheet tacked up like a back door. He look at me and Ah look at him and Ah know de two of we want to run. If Erma wasn't holding me hand again tight tight, me feet woulda been meeting de hot sand in a steady rhythm.

"Oh, Lord," he say, "Ah ain't seen one of you since me Granny died." He start to shake like hummingbird wing but he make it over to de counter bar while Erma pull me to sit down at a table by de window what so low it almost a door.

Erma leave me dere and go over and give de man a long tight hug, and dey whisper together. Den she come back and sit by me.

He breathing hard like frightened horse, but he come and stand over us with three shot glasses full of something dat look like bush tea and a bottle of Cruzan Rum. De tray rattling so in he hand de noise making me teeth chatter. Me head hurting so bad is like Ah hearing thunder, seeing fireworks, and feeling earthquake all same time.

"Drink dis," he say, "it gon' make it stop." He keep de tray rattling in he thick-skinned hands until he sit down in de frail looking stick chair.

Erma tell me dis she great uncle from she Father's side, and he gon' help me. Ah dig 'round in me bag looking for aspirin. No words ain't come to me. No words Ah could say. Only names. Louder and louder. And Ah wonder how dey ain't bust out me eyes like tears.

"Drink dis first," he say, "den if you don't feel better in two minutes you could take you pills."

He pick up a glass and full it to de brim with rum, den he extend it to me, de liquid sloshing all over de table until dere ain't but a couple of swallows left. Erma make a face as she drink hers so Ah know it gon' taste nasty. But by de time Ah rest de glass back on de tray de noise in me head lessening. Ah beginning to hear de waves from de beach and an old scratch band tune coming from de radio perched atop de bar. And Ah don't have to concentrate on keeping me head from exploding.

And den he ask me.

"How long since you get a name?"

He watching me steady. He two eyes dem cover over with de bluish screen some ole folks use to filter out what dey ain't want to see. He not shaking no more. Bright pink tongue dart out and lick he cracked lips. Fast, like lizard catch he dinner, he reach out and grab me wrist, but gentle, fingers down on de tender insides like he taking me pulse. Ah too slow to move now. A blink is like Ah sleeping.

"Un-huh, Ah see," he say, still holding me.

"What, Unc Roo?" say Erma, "what you see?" She sound like she going to cry, and Ah only see her cry two times in all dese forty-nine years since we was ten learning bamboula dance together.

"She is a Escort," he say to Erma. "She is a Escort and she don't self know it."

He holding me wrist still, and he odda hand come cover me hand and stroke it like he trying to soothe a child. Still he talking about me like Ah not dere.

Pictures scrolling through me mind like a book of postcards. Brown hands. Woman's hands. Pictures, more dan photographs, more like memories, with names across de bottom like captions. Me own hands, me own ring, what me own husband, Daniel—who living in peace and glory now twelve years already—had give me in high school, what only fit on me pinkie finger now, de gold flashing in de sun against a background of a blue knit cap covering de head dat Ah'm pressing face down in snow finer and brighter dan sand. Ah look up while Ah'm waiting for de struggling body under me to stop squirming, and Ah'm seeing a valley of green and another snow-covered mountain beyond dat. Gregory. Blue hat name is Gregory. Den is pearly pink polish on me fingernails as Ah grab de ankle of de lady in de wide

leg pants on de marble stairs. Camille. Me hands struggling to hold de steering wheel to de left as he fight to
spin it to de right. Adolfo. Me two hand dem splayed
wide wide and Ah can't even span de broad back, naked
and sweaty in de hot sun. Ah push and he fall right off
de bamboo scaffold. Lin. Fatima, at home cooking while
she mother sleeping in de next room only idly thinking
about cutting she wrists, de peevishness of a teenager,
but it's my hands dat put de force behind de knife.

Is dreams Ah tell meself. Ain't real. Too many movies. Too much TV. But Ah starting to shake and shiver
from right below me breastbone, right where me soul sit
in me body. People been calling me, calling me, calling
me. Dey names roll 'round in me head, in me mouth, like
when de boys pitching marbles and dey thumb flick de
single to break de pack. Each one different, dey scatter
with a sound like hard glass cracking, except dey don't
break, just careen off one anodda and be gone, while
anodda little group start to join and somebody, somebody with brown hands and Daniel's ring bowl into dem
and dey fly apart. Ah start to sweat and everything inside
want to come out. Ah feel Ah need to pee and coocoo
and vomit. Like Ah could void de whole of meself.

"She is a Escort, Ah tell you."

Erma watching me and smiling. She proud. Ah see it
in de way she purse she lips. Glad she bring me here so
we could get some answers. But de tears dripping, and
she squinting she eyes so she could see better when she
ask, looking from me to Uncle Roo, "So what dat mean?"

He watch me and Ah nod. Let me hear what is true.

De old man let go me hand den and pour anodda
drink of rum for each of we. Erma's eyes leaking like a
standpipe all de while.

"All right," he say, "hush up, now." So calm and slow is no more dan a whisper.

Erma reach for me, patting me back. Ah have me arms wrapped 'round me center core, holding meself together.

"You is one who does shove people across when dey ain't know it's time to go. You notice dat, right? How is always a surprise? Dey don't be sick or nothing, right?"

Me head bow down. Ah so shame.

A wave crash on de beach, and Ah hear it like it ain't past de rustling of de wild grass growing in de sandy soil, past de empty taxi with de driver door standing open while de man gone to wade since Erma tell him to wait. De wave wash me eardrums like it ain't past de lonely sea grape tree with fruit not yet ripe. Ah hear de wave. De names recede.

"How long since you get a name?"

"Three months," I tell him, "since February."

He eyes turn off den. Seem like instead of dey seeing outside of him, it's like he just turn dem 'round and he watching he own mind. A strong breeze blow through de window, and he turn he face to it slow slow, like a blind man locating a songbird. Ah watch as de wind blow a bead of sweat sideways across he cheek until it get caught up in he scraggly beard hair and make a downward turn.

"You strong," he say. "Hold out long time. But it ain't going to go until it finish. Three years is de most Ah ever hear anybody do. Den it pass, just like it come."

"Oh, God in heaven!" I call out, "in two more months I going be dead, too!"

"Okay, okay, what allyou mean? What you talking, Uncle Roo? Whatall going on?"

25

"She mubbe getting a name she insides can't let she do."

"Do? Do? What you mean do? De woman sick, not working!"

Erma bolt up and look like she gon' bust a clout on Uncle Roo. She neck veins sticking out and jumping like cold rain on a midday roof.

"Hush now, gal. I gon' tell you just now."

Uncle Roo rise up and stand tall over Erma. Erma is five eleven and does move suitcases off de ramps at de airport all day. She big, but he bigger, a long tall drink a water. Clear skin and boney. Dey watch each odda like cock in de ring, and Ah start to giggle.

De rum mubbe get me, Ah know. Ah ain't eat nothing since a piece of dumbread and tea last night. Or maybe it's dis whole thing. So stupid. So sad. I just sat dere laughing.

Even though Erma body still square off with Uncle Roo, she eyes rove over to check for me. Uncle Roo take dat as surrender and put he hand on she shoulder, pressing she to sit down. When he touch she, she flinch a little bit, but she sink so gracefully to de low chair dat it was like seeing a feather float to de ocean floor. Dat set me off again, and even as Ah thinking on big leg Erma as a feather me tears welling up, 'cause if Erma is powerless dan I mubbe gon' dead for true true.

Uncle Roo say how yes, it's work Ah doing, by taking people through death's door while Ah sleeping. How it's a job some people get, and dey just have to do it. How Ah meet up now to a name, a person, me ain't want to acknowledge and I resisting. How Ah have to do it, let meself do it, or Ah going end up doing it for real.

"What you mean, for real?" Ah ask, "Ain't real? Dese people don't die? Dey is real people anyway?" Me ain't know. Me ain't never look dem up or nothing.

"Dey real yes. You could probably find dey obituaries in dey hometown newspapers if you had dere last names. You don't though, do you? Me Granny didn't get last names. But me Granny's was all from 'round here. People she know. Dat was real hard on her, she feel guilty all de time, she tell me, until she find someone dat know what going on, like you find me."

Ah nod me head. Is like de line in de ole Lord Pretender song, "somebody suffering more dan you."

"So now you mubbe get a name of somebody you know, and if you ain't do it de way it's 'posed to be done, den you gon' do it in you waking hours and it going to be worse for everybody."

Erma mouth hanging open, catching flies, but Ah know what he mean. Is like me brain take a breath. I feel relieved. Like when you food ain't digest and it sitting on your heart, den somebody pat you on your back, give you some comfort and it move off.

Uncle Roo rise up and go off into de back room. We hear him moving things and making noise like he straining, until finally he come back with a green glass bottle with a cork stopper. He dust de thing off with he pant leg, rolling it 'round on he thighs. I could see de insides swirling 'round, mixing what probably ain't been disturbed in twenty years.

"You must drink dis," he say, putting de bottle directly in me bag, "tonight. You must bathe in painkiller bush bath, and clothe youself in something white. Drink dis right at you bedside, right after you get up off you knees. De whole thing. It taste all right. Won't make you sick or nothing neida. When you wake up, de blockage be gone and you could move on."

Is my eyes leaking now. I so grateful for de help. Erma pulling me up with one hand and rooting in she purse with de odda. Uncle Roo backing away like is now he seeing ghosts.

"Uh-uh," he say, "don't try to give me nothing, Erma, or you neida. Just do what Ah say and come tell me everything is just so in two months when you feeling better."

Is more dan tears now, me chest heaving and me sobs sounding like conch horn. Nobody ain't have to call back de taxi man, he come running and we get into de car and be gone.

I never even get to drink de tonic. It gone to de bottom of de sea.

It happen when we were leaving de ferry boat. De boat tie up to de pier, and we walking down de board plank to de dock. De white lady ahead of Erma slip, and she scream and flail 'round trying to right sheself. Erma jump when she hear de scream and I jump too, and me pocketbook sway into Erma's backside and dat startle she even more. Ah remember like Ah living it again. Like Ah living it for both of we. She was holding on to de rope guide with she left hand. One a de boatman, four people in front to de right, all blinding in he white shirt and white pants, steadying people as dey crossing over. Wasn't nobody close behind Erma but me. When me pocketbook swing and slap she butt she reach to swat it away, just while she body was still reacting to de woman scream, just when she release she weight from she left leg for she next step on she right. She right knee buckle and she crumple right down on she hands and knees. She tip right over, sideways, and as she falling, she unfolding, like a paper fan. With a pow Erma hit de water, lengthwise, between de dock and de slimy green of de boat sides. She legs and body sink right under while she head remain aloft. I grab de rope thing with me two hand and let me body slide down into de water feet first. But Ah too late. Ah know it's de waves making de boat and de dock knock together, but what really happen is de sea take a deep breath and on de inhale Mami Water contract everything tight, tight, de boat and de dock, Erma's ribs and Erma's lungs, and like day and night does meet, so life and death had meet in me sweet friend Erma. When Ah reach face to face with Erma in de water, she rum breath expel into me face and Ah breathe it in for me own. Red spit bubbles come out she mouth, and she stare at me hard with she eyes wide in question, like de time I give she de plane ticket to Puerto Rico for she Christmas and she watch me like I make mistake. I brace me arms aside she breasts, under she arms, holding she up, trying to keep de knocking of de boat from reaching she. Blow after blow landing on me back as de ferry rocking with de waves, but Ah know she dying already, right here in me arms. Right here in de sea.

De hospital tell me me two legs crush like matchsticks, and me arms and shoulders all mash up from holding back de ferry. But Erma's body not broke, except for where she ribs had puncture she lungs in Mami Water's first embrace.

Ah dreaming a name every night again. And me ain't feel like me soul hiccupping. Ah know I have more names to go, but Ah do de hardest one already.

The Dreamprice

Dis bank been here donkey years an' dey still ain't got nowhere ta park. Six measly spots. What' day call dat? Convenience? I call it rude. Jus' inconsiderate an' outta place. Now looka dis. Looka dis woman, no? Wha' she tink I sittin here fo' if not waitin fo' dat space?! I feel ta go ovah dere an' tell she 'bout she tiefin' self. Eh, eh. I losin' it. S'pose ta be watchin' me pressure. Tings hard 'nough widout takin' on all dese triflin' people wha' don' know no better. Lea' she have de space. She don' got it anyway. She prob'ly need it mo' dan me. But who t'is could need it mo' dan me? Wid dese heels on, in dis heat, wid thirty-seven cents ta me name. Who? I wouldn'ta even have ta be here, if weren't fo' dat loose brain chile a mine. Derecia never know where she foot gon' land when she pick it up. Come telling me dis morning' she need twenty dollars, me last money, fo' de SAT test at school. Dis selfsame mornin'! She had know 'bout de test, musta had dat form in she bag fo' de last tree weeks by de looks a it. Oh, good, dere's a space. 'Bout time. An' I have ta go ta de bathroom so bad, but look a de time already. I can' stop now.

No sooner dan I walk inta de bank do I hear me name bein' bawl out inna way I wa' taught not ta answer. Deep in de crowd, 'bout twenty-fifth in line it look like ta me, I see a tounchy liddle ol' lady, no bigger dan a upright iguana, wid a smile as warm an' friendly lookin' as a tub a hot water fo' me achin' feet. An' she just a flaggin' me down wid a pocketbook so humongous I didn't see how she coulda lift it ovah she head.

"Lorraine! Lorraine! Lorraine Meyers! Girl, you put on weight. Come ovah here! Let me get a good look at you!"

Who da is? I know dat lady. Who she is? Who is she?

"Good afternoon, Ma'am. How are you today?" I say. I have ta pass her close 'cause she on de outside a de line. Oh, yeah, she use ta be one a Mommy friends, Mrs. Witherspun. Now why she gotta go call attention ta me weight?

"Well, Lorraine. It's been quite a while since I seen you, I don't get out too much no more. So how's your Mommy?"

She wangle dat suitcase a her'n up on she shoulder an' grab ahold a me hand.

"Mommy died, Mrs. Witherspun," I say, "almost two years ago. But thank you for asking."

"She did what? You gotta speak up, I don't hear like I used to. She did what you say?"

"I said, my mother passed away, Mrs. Witherspun. But thank you for asking."

I try ta pull away. She pull me back.

"She did? Passed on? Nobody told me."

She start massagin' me hand. I tink she tink she tryna say she sorry fo' not knowin' an' sorry fo' bringin' it up an' sorry fo' makin' me repeat it, but it only makin' me have ta go ta de bathroom worse.

"When?"

"Two years ago next month" I say, tuggin' at me hand.

"About two years ago you say. I musta been off island. I so sorry to hear dat. We were de best of friends for years. Long rolling years, up until she went and….well, she was quite a woman, your Mommy. What you say she died of, eh, sweetheart?"

"If you don' mind, Mrs. Witherspun, I rather not talk 'bout it right now. An I have ta get on line if I ever gon' get outta here dis afternoon. It was nice—"

"Now, don't run off, Lorraine. Here, you can get on line right here in front of me. We can catch up. Dese nice people won't mind. Unhook dat thing," she commanded.

She mince backwards four, five feet widout raisin' she heels from de floor. De elder gentleman in back a she try not ta yield, but as she almos' leanin' on him, an' he as skinny as a papaya tree in de first place, back he went. I look ovah de faces a de people 'round us, hopin' fo' some belligerent fool ta get me outta dis situation an' who do I see but one a Derecia's teachers. Wha' she doin' here dis time a day? An' ain't dat Tyrone? Eh, eh. Jus' wha' I need. Me boyfriend Leon's fool friend. I hope *he* don' say nothin'.

So I went in. Mrs. Witherspun wait quietly while I unhook de velvet rope and latch it back behind me. I felt like I wa' stealin'. Stealin' odda people time. I didn't z'actly get in front a she an' turn me back, but I stood kinda sideways an' start lookin' busy in me bag.

"Thank you," I say.

"Well, Ellie's gone. I can't hardly believe it. I liked her. She was different from me, of course. But still, we was gals together. For years. Long rolling years. Did she ever quit smoking and drinking? She was de same age as me. What happen to her? T'was a accident? I hope Ellie died peacefully."

"She did, Mrs. Witherspun. As peacefully as possible." Den I tink dat ain' such a nice ting ta say ta a ol' lady who mubbe polishin' death's doorknob.

"Was she in de hospital?" she ask.

But she jus' don' give up.

"Yes, Mrs. Witherspun, just for a little while," I say.

"I hope dey was good to her. Sometimes hospitals can be de wrong place to be when you in pain. Was she in pain, Lorraine?"

I tryin' not ta get upset. I still have ta pee. I can' find me pen an' me feet startin' ta throb.

"Mrs. Witherspun," I say, "Mommy died a liver cancer, in de hospital, after four months a bein' sick. But she restin' now an' I glad you remember her fondly." Dere, I tink I did good.

"Of course I remember her. We used to have a ball together. She was always leading me off to watch her get in trouble. A pretty woman, too. Always kept herself up. How's your father?"

"Me father?"

"Yes, your father. Ellie use ta be crazy 'bout him! T'was a pity dey could never marry. Ellie used ta cry so 'bout dat. How is he?"

He ain' close enough ta hell. But a course me ain' say dat.

"He's in Tradewinds," I say.

"What you say?"

I tryin'ta whisper, we in a bank an' all, but as she half deaf an' I half a foot taller dan she, t'ain gon' work.

"He in de Tradewinds Nursing Home, Mrs. Witherspun." Dis time I do turn me back.

"What you say?" She inch forward an' put she bony hand on me arm an' turn me back ta face her. "Roland? Roland De Rascal being cared for in de Tradewinds Nursing Home? By strangers? I don't believe it. How come?"

"I don't know," I mumble.

"Wha'cha mean, yoh ain' know? You his daughter, ain't you? Everybody know dat," she wave she arm, indicatin' everybody dat was listenin' I guess, "even if you ain't got his name." She suck her teeth an' step back, distancin' herself from me. "Umph, umph, umph," she say.

Did I lea' de whole ting drop dey?? No. I jump back in.

"Mrs. Widaspun," an' me ain' botherin' ta whispa no mo', "dat man was no kinda Farda ta me an' nothin' but trouble ta me Mudda neida."

"But you sound so bitter, chile. He was jus' a man. He tried ta do right by you, much as he could, under de circumstances, you know, wid him being married an' all. Why, I remember he use ta take you out for your every birthday. Now, didn't he, Lorraine?"

I wish I coulda suck me teeth. "He took me out one time. One time, Mrs. Widaspun, when I was fourteen."

"Oh, yes, I remember dat time." She liddle body make dese spastic motions, an' I could hardly believe she wa' laughin'. "You was 'bout fourteen, right? He almost lost you inna pool game!" She laugh. "Or was it dominos? At one of dem houses!" She laugh. "De rascal! Your Mommy was plenty vex wid him den. I remember. Still, Tradewinds? Lorraine, we all make mistakes."

I wanted ta tell she dat he had make 'leven odda mistakes jus' like me an' had six chil'ren from he wife at home an' ain' do right by none a we. But I wasn' raise ta be rude so I jus' say, "Excuse me, Mrs. Witherspun, I can't find my pen so I goin' go use de one on de counter."

"You don't have to, child, I have one right here." She start rummagin' in she bag. "Dem chains dey got those things on never do be long enough no way. Here, here you go. Black ink. Just like dey like it."

I took de pen an' start searchin' 'round in me pocketbook.

"Oh, Lorraine, guess what? I been standing here
tryin' to remember why I was so happy to see you, today
of all days, aside from de fact dat I ain' seen you in so
long and all a dat and it just came back to me."

Oh, Lord, I tink, shiftin' me weight, what next?

"I had a dream about you."

Me stomach lurch up an' me palms start ta sweat an'
I almos' broke me water right dere on de line.

"You know 'bout my dreams, don't you, Lorraine?
Dey come true. Well, not all of dem. But I can tell. And
this one. This one dat I had last night. 'Bout you. It was
one of dem."

Good or bad? Good or bad? Me mind feel like a dog
dat had eat hot peppers an' is barkin' and strainin' on
he chain.

"Mrs. Witherspun, you have to excuse me, I must
find a restroom. Now."

I unhook de velvet rope latch an' lea' it jus' so as I
waddle away. I sure I waddlin' 'cause me ain' wan' take too
long a stride. Me pocketbook hangin' open and bouncin'
on me hip. Every slap a de leather make me wan' cry, but
I so undone I can' even find de sense enough ta close it.
I know where de bathroom is, an' I know it ain' fo' customers, but I don' care. I goin' in.

Afterwards, after, I tryin' catch meself, but I wan'
jump up an' down an' scream, de way Pookie does
do when you turn de TV away from Sesame Street. I
thought 'bout takin' me shoes off, but was 'fraid it'd
hurt too much ta get dem back on. Told meself dat Mrs.
Witherspun was just a lonely ol' lady who didn't always

remember tings right, an' I shouldn't be pissed at her 'cause she spreadin' me business in de street.

I put on fresh lipstick.

Mommy had tell me dat one time Mrs. Witherspun had a dream 'bout de Governor. He wasn't governor den. Only a teenager. Dey was all 'round de same age. She was so sure of dis one dream dat she wrote it all down, even de parts she didn't understand, an' seal dem in envelopes an' send dem all ovah de place. But he ain' pay her no mind, say she crazy, he goin' ta be a musician. Some kinda horn, I tink. Saxophone maybe. Well she tell he he must never marry some girl. I forget she name. Said even though he would love her, he better not marry her, no matter what. Forty something odd years later, when he start campaignin', Mrs. Witherspun pull out she letters. Later on, when he give his inauguration speech she understand 'bout de train. Obviously, he ain' marry her, whosoever she was. Don' know why doh, probably had nothin' ta do wid dat. But still, some people do see tings. Good or bad? Never mind. Me ain' wan' know, I say. I can do widout knowin'. I don' have ta know. I goin' back outside, get on de end a de line an' forget 'bout dis, dat an' Miss Wither-Big-Mouth-Won't-Mind-She-Own-Business-spun. Now dat I don' have ta pee, I can wait forever.

I try not ta look. Try ta amble on ovah behind dis fat lady, but I hear she callin' me name, jus' like befo'. De line had hardly move. I couldn't ignore she 'cause everybody on line already knew me damn name.

"Lorraine, I saved your space for you. You knew I would. You so humble, child. I like dat. You just come right back here. Dese nice people don't mind."

De nice people wave me through. I feel like a football player. You know when dey does do de roll call an' all a dem does get a pat on de behind befo' dey da go out dere an' jump 'pon one 'nother?

"So, Lorraine, you feel better now? Good. Good. I know you got a bad bladder. I remember, you didn't quit wetting de bed 'til you was almost seventeen."

I hear 'bout nine different laughs up an' down de line. Hee. Hee. Hah. Hah. Ho. Ho. Including Derecia's teacher an' Leon's friend, Tyrone an' Papaya Tree wid his scruffy headed self.

Don' take it on, I tell meself. Dat was years ago. An' wha' she know? I started wid me pocketbook again. Nine. I was nine.

"So, anyway, like I was saying, I had a dream about you last night. A very special dream."

"Oh, yeah? A good dream, I hope." I tryna act like I ain' really interested. Tryin' not ta be interested. Let's see, I tink, today is Tuesday, an' I don't get me check 'til Thursday, an' I gotta put gas in de car, at least fifteen dollars, an' go ta de laundry, dat's another fifteen, an' Ameka goin' on a field trip wid she class, an' I tink she say eight, so I need at least—

"Lorraine! Lorraine! Turn 'round here and look at me when I'm talking to you! Your Mommy didn't drag you up through no gutter!"

I drop me hands ta me sides instantly. "No, Ma'am. I'm sorry, Ma'am."

"Uh huh," say Papaya Tree.

"People pay good money to hear my dreams, you know."

"Yes, Ma'am."

"And I'm telling you your dream, fresh, from last night, for free."

"Yes, Ma'am."

"Humph," she say.

Papaya was 'bout ta say so too, but I sorta look at him sideways, not z'actly outta de corner a me eye, but kinda, an' he ain' say nothin'. Tyrone back dere laughin'.

"Now, do you want to hear it or don'tcha?"

"Yes, Mrs. Witherspun, please do tell me 'bout your dream, Ma'am," I say.

De whole line sigh. I swear, everybody on line seem ta exhale at de same damn time.

"Well, pay attention den, and don't interrupt."

"Yes, Ma'am."

I stand quietly, humbly, waitin'. Mrs. Witherspun didn't say nothin' for a l-o-n-g time. I start ta inch me hand toward me pocketbook ta get me checkbook, but when dose chickenhawk eyes catch sight a de movement she humph again. So dere I is, wid me hand at half mast, tryna look all eager an' grateful while Mrs. Witherspun soakin' up me contrition.

Finally she begin. Loud? "Well, it started with you, Lorraine. In bed. All sweaty. Hair all messed up. In bed with—"

She stop. De ol' nanny goat jus' stop. What Mommy do dis lady make she wan' treat me so? Tyrone cup he hand behind he one good ear, 'fraid it weren't workin' right. Two noisy schoolgirls join de line an' somebody, me ain' know who, I tink t'was de teacher, but I don' know, somebody, actually shush dem.

Oh, Lord, I tink. Wha' kinda day is dis?

"You was in bed with a fever." I practically had ta read she lips, so low she say dis part.

Mommy send she, I tink, send she ta wrought up me nerves.

"Wasn't AIDS or nothin'," she blastin' now, you know, "but you was talkin' all outta your head. Delirious, you know. Wid de fever. Cryin' and carryin' on about Raymond. You remember Raymond, don'tcha? Course you do. He's your boy's daddy. Gerald. Right? Well you was justa yellin' about "don't go, Raymond, don't go." I sure you was tryna keep him from goin' back in de trailer. Remember? Course you do. Dat was when you and him had run off to live together."

She actually turn 'round an' speak ta Papaya Tree.

"Dey was only in high school," she say. "You believe dat?"

She turn back ta me. "Anyway, dat was when your Mommy had put you out. Can't say I blame her, as disgraceful as you was behaving and all. And her boyfriend, what was his name? He didn't last long. But still he was important. What was his name, Lorraine?"

His name was Maxworth General. I could picture him clear clear in me mind.

"Maxworth."

"Yes, dat's right. Maxworth. Anyway, he, Maxworth, he's de one dat rent allyou some empty trailer he had at de edge of de parking lot. You remember? Of course you remember. And allyou was just snotty teenagers, too. Setting up house. Humph. Least allyou stayed in school. Course dey didn't know you was pregnant den, yet, did dey? De school I mean. 'Cept how dey didn't figure it out what wid Raymond making a baby crib in woodshop class and all, I don't know. Still, people had a way a minding dey own business. You remember? Anyway it was dere dat Raymond died, right? Tryin' to get de baby crib outta de trailer de night it caught fire. Right?"

Right! Right! Shut up, no?!

"So, so anyway, you was bawling for Raymond to not go back in. Said you didn't want to take de chance. Let de crib burn. Allyou was safe and on and on you went and I saw de fire and everything, in de dream, or nightmare, or whatever, and…and it was just horrible! Horrible, right, Lorraine? And you was doin' all kinda thrashin' on de bed, but dat was in de dream. I remember de real life too. Not you, but your poor Mommy. She liked to drink herself to death in de next few months. She liked Raymond so, said he was coming to be such a good man, working so hard to take care of you."

"Mommy said?"

"Yes, your Mommy. She knew he loved you and woulda take good care a you. But allyou was just too young! Too young to be jumpin' up in de face of love. Shamin' people. But you wouldn't know dat, now would you? How your Mommy was hurting? You was too busy being mean and spiteful, now wasn't you?"

Spiteful? Is dat how Mommy saw it? I had me own grief ta deal wid. An' she had put me out, an' cuss me stink, hadn't she, jus' two months befo'? An' she had like Raymond? She never tell me dat. Not in all de years after, neida, she never tell me dat.

"Well, you was carrying on so, in de dream, you know, dat you woke your ownself up and you went straight to your vanity—you got a vanity, Lorraine?"

I felt like I had jus' drink sour milk. Why t'is dat when you need your mind clear your body does go on de attack?

"Lorraine?!"

"What?" Me ain' mean ta answer her so, it just come out.

"Don't you answer me with no what! Now, I asked you if you got a vanity."

"Yes, Ma'am." Vanity?

"I thought so. And is it white?"

"Yes. Ma'am." Raymond. Raymond. Mommy. Of course I remember.

"And does it have four legs or not?"

Wha' she talkin' 'bout? "Excuse me, Mrs. Widaspun," I say, "wha' you say?"

Den Papaya Tree say, "Mrs. Witherspun means to say, does it have a solid back wid just two legs in de front, or is it more like a table wid four legs?"

"Like a table wid four legs," I say, wid me head swivelin' from pillar ta post 'cause I don' know who I s'pose ta answer.

We move forward in line, couldn'ta been de first time, but t'was de only time I had ta actually *move* me body, you know?

"I knew it. I know just what it looks like. Saw it in my dream. So anyway, you went straight to your vanity, and of course you saw your hair all messed up and you was lookin' terrible and you turned this way and dat, lookin' at yourself, and right den and dere you said you was goin' into business for yourself."

"Good for you," says Papaya.

Business? Wha' I know 'bout business?

"What kind of business, Mrs. Witherspun?"

"A salon," she say.

"A beauty salon?" Well now, I never thought a dat.

"No. No. De other one den. A saloon. You know, where dey sell gin and rum and such."

"A rum shop?!"

Tyrone hollered. I recognized de sound, de mixed up bongs of a fog horn an' a church bell. But Papaya come ta me defense.

"Don' laugh," he say, four people back ta Tyrone," dey make a lot of money."

"Yes, dey do," says Mrs. Witherspun, "and anyway, it was more like a bar. Or maybe a bar and a restaurant. Anyway dere was liquor."

"Where I get de money ta start dis business, Mrs. Witherspun?"

"From your son. Dat bad boy of yours, by Raymond. Gerald. He's de one dat's de gangster, right? Must be about twenty, right?"

"He ain' no gangster an' he twenty-two!" I yellin' now.

"Well," she yellin' back, "he don' work! Ain' nebber work! Yoh his Mudda and his daddy dead! Yet an' all he come up wid thirty-five thousand dollars and dere yoh was! In business! Yoh wanna tell me where he get it from?!"

"He ain' no gangster."

"Whatever," she say, like it ain' important.

We getting' nearer ta de head a de line. I get out me checkbook an' write meself a check. Den I turns back ta Mrs. Witherspun, I done come dis far already, an' I say, "So was de business successful, Mrs. Witherspun?"

"Yes, dear, you made lots of money."

"Anyting else I should know?"

"Oh, so you believe me now?" she say, eyin' me up and down. If she weren't so ol' I'da put she in she place good!

"I don' doubt dat your dreams often come true, Mrs. Witherspun," I say, hopin' dat's enough.

"Humph!"

"Me Mudda told me de one about de Governor."

"Dat was a long time ago. This one's fresh."

"Yes," I say. An' I done. Dat's as far as I goin'.

"So, anyway, she say, "den you got married."

Well! I nearly fall ovah on de flo'. Try grab ahold a de velvety ting, but a course dat ain' stable me and I stumble 'round a good while. Married? Me? Wha' de hell fo'?

"Dat's right. You married some fella with white hair."

Leon????

"And you was happy, too. Wasn't like when you was common law with dat odda fella, what's his name? Ameka's father. De one dat used to cuff you up. Or was dat Pookie's father? How is Pookie, by de way? Now, she's a sweetheart. No. No. Her father was de good-looking man from de church, right? De minister? Or was he a deacon? Must be de hand a God in dat child, she so precious. Not like dat other girl you got. Derecia. Who is her father anyway? I can never remember. Anyway, you was married. Good and legal."

T'was my turn ta go up ta de teller an' I jus' turn off. But Mrs. Witherspun yell afta me.

"What's de matter with you? You should be happy!" She took she place at de teller next ta mine an' continue.

"You got your own money so you could finally get off welfare—"

"Disability!" I shouts. Is disability fo' me back.

But Mrs. Witherspun ignore me an' present she bankbook ta de teller wid a formal an' dignified soundin', "Good afternoon, Miss," den she turn back ta me an' yell, "an' somebody finally marry you! Dat's more'n you ever had. And I see it comin'. In my dream. You should be happy!"

Me ain' say a mumblin' word.

We finish at de same time an' you know wha' de ol' snake tongue iguana say ta me? Softly, all quiet an' secretive? Afta she done wrung me out an' spread me wide?

Fo' a rum shop an' a marriage license?! Liddle iguana say, "Lorraine? Lorraine? I got something to ask you. I need a favor. I know you'll do it for me, being your Mommy child and all. But I don't want to ask you here, in de street. Let's go somewhere private, okay? You understand. Come."

An' jus' like dat, all of a sudden, I had ta pee again.

Mrs. Littleson's Recollection

I used to do these girls. Their mother brought them on alternating Saturday mornings for a press and curl. The older one, she wasn't bad, sat quietly and behaved herself. She had a lot of hair, hair thick as thieves, late for school hair. The little one though, reminded me of a squirrel. She never kept still. A bony child, too, with knees like castanets. If she wasn't so bowlegged she'd be her own rhythm section.

This particular Saturday the mother brings the young one to me at ten o'clock. She's going to be my fourth of the day and my last before lunch. I'm just curling up Miss Aggie's garden peas and she's so still I think she must be praying. Maryleen is sitting at the vanity that I have set up for people like her, primping herself to the nnth degree. She's been saying that she's almost done for fifteen minutes, and I've been finished with her for over an hour. She's not bothering me though. We're just chatting while Miss Aggie's praying and I'm dripping puddles of sweat on the floor. Maryleen's taking her time fixing herself up, plucking her eyebrows, soaking her nails, and pushing her cuticles. Me, I don't have time to hold anyone's hand.

"Beauty takes time," Maryleen says to me in her soft voice that sounds like the hiss of the hot iron.

"Amen," says Miss Aggie, back from wherever she's been.

"That's true," I say, spinning Miss Aggie around so she'll realize she's finished. She doesn't get a comb out. Miss Aggie is one of those people that like a thing to last. She sticks two fat fingers in the knot of her white handkerchief and comes up with a folded piece of cloth about an inch square. She unleashes this thing, and it's almost as big as a tablecloth. She ties this around her curls without messing them up as me and Maryleen and the bony child and the bony child's mother watch. Then she pokes around in her handkerchief again and pulls up what I've been waiting for. My money.

"God bless you, Vera," she says to me as she slides the money in my apron pocket as if I'm not supposed to touch it. I always think one of these days I'm going to reach in my pocket and find a one dollar bill grinning at me. Then I'll be forced to forget my home training. But Miss Aggie isn't like that, my thoughts just wander foolishly and I usually go for the ride.

"Good morning, Mrs. Littleson," the child's mother says to me again, as if she didn't say it when she came in ten minutes ago. She's Mrs. Muckedymuck, and her husband is Mr. Muckedymuck eating high off the government hog.

"Good morning," I say back. She's nice enough. And a good customer too, never asks for credit or anything. The girl, meanwhile, is inching forward on feet big enough to float a boat.

Maryleen stands up. That's one woman I have never seen slouching or leaning. She's as straight as a pine tree, but not as stiff, moves with ease and grace. Her flesh, and Maryleen has flesh all over, looks as firm as a young bride's, which I know she isn't. She smoothes her dress down, and the wrinkles at her hips disappear at her command.

She wiggles her feet into her shoes next, toenails all shiny with pearly pink polish. She takes a step forward and turns her back to the mirror to check the seam of her dress. It falls straight and divides her behind exactly in half.

The child examines Maryleen from her pointy-toed shoes all the way up to her upswept hair three or four times, grinning so hard I can see down her throat straight to her breakfast.

Maryleen smiles at the little squirrel. "It's your turn now, honey," she says, "Mrs. Littleson will fix you up good." She comes and gives me my money and sashays out the door.

Maybe the child will sit still today I think, but she throws herself in the chair like a sack of dry bones and I think not. Her mother watches me while I drape her in a fresh cloth.

"You staying here today, ma'am?" I ask. She usually goes about her business and comes back to pick her up. She's usually on time, too, except for once when the girl was here until after four o'clock.

She springs up from her chair and says no, she's going to run some errands and will be back soon.

"Fine," I say, "We'll be right here when you get back."

"Bye, Mommy," the girl hollers, even though her mother is only four feet away.

"Bye-bye Leslie," her mother says, "don't give Mrs. Littleson a hard time."

No wonder I can never remember the child's name. Had a boy in my school named Leslie, he kissed me on the cheek one day, and I swear I got a wart the next.

Whispering now, while her mother clacks down the steps, the child, Leslie, says, "Mrs. Littleson?"

"Yes?" I answer, just as sweet as I can be, hot and tired as I am. I'm adjusting the water. She doesn't like it too hot.

"Mrs. Littleson, I don't want you to burn me today, okay?"

Well. I fling the girl back in the chair and slam the chair down on the neck rest. The child's eyes bug out more than usual.

"Humph."

I make her stay like that while I loosen her wild braids and rub her scalp. When the water hits her, and it's hot now, you know, she closes her eyes tight, but she doesn't move. I remind myself that she's just a child, eight, nine, ten, around there.

"Pride feels no pain," I say to her, loud enough for her to hear over the water I have rushing in her big ears.

"Pride feels no pain, Leslie," I say again, "Hasn't your mother ever told you that?"

"No, Mrs. Littleson," she says.

"Miss Maryleen sure is beautiful, isn't she?" I ask when the steam of the hot comb hits her scalp for the first time. I never burned her. Never burned anybody. It's the steam that gets them.

I do her hair differently that day, with drop curls in the back and bangs. Hope her mother doesn't mind, but with a forehead like that she needs to wear bangs all the time.

"Ooooh!" she says when I let her see herself in the mirror.

"That looks real nice, now doesn't it? That wasn't so bad, now, was it?" I say. She just looks. And she's still looking when her mother comes in a few minutes later while I'm tidying up and thinking about my lunch and all the heads I have to do this afternoon.

"Look, Mommy," the child screams, sounding like she has the lungs of a donkey. Her mother smiles and tells her how pretty she looks and all that. Then she pays me, and the child, who's been coming here for about two years, doesn't need to be told to say thank you.

"Thank you, Mrs. Littleson," she says, looking me in the baby of my eyes, real serious.

"You're welcome, Miss Leslie," I say. Sweetly. After all, she's just a child.

One clacks and the other stomps down the stairs.

"Mommy, Mrs. Littleson says pride feels no pain. Do you believe that?" the child asks when they're on the street. Her mother was a pretty and well-put-together lady, so I figured she'd say yes.

"My mother told me that, too," Mrs. Muckedymuck says, "Yes, I believe it, do you?"

"Yes, I do!" she brays, threatening to toss her big head off her bony neck.

"Humph," I say as I latch the door, "she shouldn't give me any more trouble."

That was almost twenty years ago. I haven't done her since she was about seventeen, but she was in town last week. Came and kissed and hugged me. She looks good, isn't bony any more either. Told me she hasn't combed her hair in nine years and was proud of it. Has those locs or dreads or whatever they call them hanging all down her back. I asked her why she went and did a thing like that, and she said her hair is her way of representing the beauty of Black women. Said it takes the same amount of work and care as straightened hair, but makes her feel like her beauty is her own, authentic, not an imitation. She still doesn't wear bangs. Hair must have grown where there wasn't any before, because she looks all right. Actually, she looks very good.

Same amount of work, huh? I never thought about it before, but maybe I better look into this. I thought it was a fad or a passing trend but it seems like it's here to stay, these locs. I'm a businesswoman, I may have to make some adjustments.

Another thing she said, that Leslie, she told me she does have pride, but would bear her pain some other way. Humph. Wonder what way is that?

Stuck

I'm being nice, doing my work, telling everybody to have a blessed day when bam! All of sudden I want to slap my boss and stab her in the thigh with a paper clip. She's the type of woman who wants me to respond to each and every damn piece of junk mail and sales call that crosses her horizon. I'm the type of woman who'll throw it all away.

So you can imagine my surprise when I get raptured up to heaven with a bent paper clip and a murderous attitude.

First of all, heaven ain't white. Or blue either. It's green. Lots and lots of green. Baby puke green. Split pea soup green. So much green it makes me nauseous. And there're snakes, too. It's a little too warm, and the whole set-up looks like a Hollywood Garden of Eden. I'm not too happy about this. It's half an hour past lunch time already.

I turn around. Looking for a door I must have come through. A hole in the ground. Exit sign. Something. I do *not* have time to play around in Hollywood.

I'm getting ready to take two steps forward and faint when I hear a voice with more bass than Barry White.

"What are you doing here?"

I always wanted to faint.

And now would have been a good time since it appears that the iridescent blue snake with the green eyes and fake purple eyelashes is talking to me. Rudely.

"You don't belong here either," I say, looking down at the cobra wanna-be with the glued-on blond weave, "so don't give me any lip."

"I belong wherever I am. I've been blessed like that."

I suck my teeth, "Well, bless me with the way outta here."

"I ask you again. What are you doing here?" She slithers closer to me, keeping her tail end high off the ground so she doesn't lose her gold bangles.

"I don't know," I admitted.

"Well, you'll just have to wait then."

"Wait for what?"

But she was gone.

And wait, I did.

At first I wasn't just waiting. I was yelling. I was stomping around. I was searching for a way out. Didn't feel like heaven to me. But there was a big sign. Said "HEAVEN. WAIT HERE."

None of the other snakes would talk to me. The birds either. I waited. The light changed. I guessed the sun was going down. Or however it happened here. I worried. Worried that the boss would think I'd quit and then I'd get fired. Worried that my son Jabari might have forgotten his key again and wouldn't remember that his sister Janelle was supposed to be at the library until he picked her up at six o'clock. Worried that no one would take the dog out and they'd all step over and around his business until I got home to clean it up. Worried that my husband wouldn't feed the children until sometime after my memorial service. Wouldn't make sense to have a funeral with no body in the casket since, well, since my body was obviously……here.

I exhausted myself pulling and pushing everything that looked like it could move. With my paper clip I poked and picked on anything that looked like it wouldn't bite. Finally I sat down under a tree. I don't know what kind of tree. Brown trunk, green leaves. The kind you see in a park. I sat for so long I wondered why my butt wasn't numb. Why I wasn't hungry. I felt exactly the same as I had when I wanted to stab my boss in the thigh.

After a few billion years, Miz bedecked and bejeweled came back. I was actually happy to see her. She lowered herself from a branch above me, being careful not to lose her jewelry. Red weave this time, same eyelashes. Diamond earrings, hanging off her, what'dya call those things? Look like labia to me.

"You're still here?" she asks.

How can a snake smirk?

I rolled my eyes. I had wanted answers and company and a way out, but her attitude pissed me off. Some people say I'm too sensitive.

"What are you doing?"

"I'M WAITING!" I yelled. I hadn't really meant to yell. "Waiting."

"Not here, stupid. Over there. Where it says…uh… 'wait here.' "

This time she didn't disappear, just wound herself back up into the tree. I heard her up there chuckling, but I refused to move.

Cheap looking sign. Sloppy red spray paint on a torn bed sheet, strung up between ladders of different sizes with frayed clothesline. Heaven, my ass.

I decided to go stand under the sign. Directly under it? Facing it? In back of it? What? So picky around here.

As I get near it, I'm not there anymore. I feel all warm and wet, and between one blink and the next I find myself in a bubble bath. It's nice and all, but unnecessary and uncalled for. The room is pink. Everything is pink. The tub, the ceiling, the walls. Candlelit. Looks like a frigging sunset. Feels like the Twilight Zone. I grab the sides of the tub and struggle to rise. The bottom is slippery, and even though I can't see past the bubbles it feels like there're fish in here.

There's a towel. Pink. I wrap it around me without drying off. Not that I'm particularly hideous. Or shy.

"Delores?"

Is that God calling me?

"Delores, will you come out here now?"

Can't be God. Sounds like my Uncle Max.

Door. Doorknob. Not pink. Yes I'm ready to go out there. I need to get this mess over with. Get on with life, damn it.

I would like to wrap the towel around my chest and tuck it closed, but I'm a little too big for that so I settle for holding it with one hand and opening the door with the other. For once I'm glad that I'm not taller, or the towel wouldn't be much more than a cummerbund.

But I guess God has already seen me naked.

And for that matter, so has Uncle Max.

It is Uncle Max. Spitting image. Right down to the two-toned shoes. And those long, long fingers with the jagged fingernails.

I wasn't frightened before, but now I am. I clutch the towel so tightly against my chest I can feel my heart beating against my fist.

"Hey there, Decidedly Sweet Delores. How are you?"

"Uncle Max? I thought you were God. Were gonna be God. Was gonna be…God."

"God? No Baby Girl. I'm not God. He sent me though. Come here and give your old Uncle some sugar. I haven't seen you since…well, you know, since you were a damn sight thinner and younger." He laughs, reaching out for me. I can smell his Old Spice cologne from here.

I try to back up. I know I hadn't actually taken a step forward. Out of the pink room with the tub. I'd just opened the door. But there's no doorknob in my hand. There's nothing. Nothing but the stupid paper clip between me and Uncle Max.

I guess I'm tuning out. I only hear snatches of what he's saying. He hasn't moved and neither have I.

"……God told me…I know all about what happened to you…. I know in third grade no one would play with you anymore after you wet your pants at recess…. I know that when you were ten you saw Mrs. Matlin throw her dog out the tenth story window…that your mother told everyone your older brother was the last child she should have had…when I came along…you were such a sad-looking child…you knew that girl was just using you to do her homework…you smiled when I tickled you… teenage boys are fickle, you know that…she didn't mean nothing by it…may have been a little harsh, but was only trying…expect her to stand up to the principal to save you…you've got such pretty eyes…I never meant…instead…and now look at you…so take it out on me…"

I heard that part. I clearly heard that part. I took a step toward Uncle Max and he backed up. I took another step and so did he. I rushed him and we crashed down. For the first time I was on top and I stuck him right under his chin with my paper clip. I stuck him again and again and again, moving down his torso, sitting on his thighs, his shins, until he sounded like a room full of dying balloons. He never fought. He never even looked at me. His eyes were closed the whole time. But still it was satisfying.

After I caught my breath I got up off his deflated legs and looked around for my towel. I reached down to pick it up and when I straightened up I was back in the Garden of Hollywood Heaven.

Miz Bejeweled was right there looking up at me.

"What do you see now?" she says, bright red shiny lip gloss on her no-lip-having-self, trying to look all smug.

I'm mad now. Still mad. At least I think I am. But I don't actually feel mad. I just feel tired. Arm aches a little.

"What does the sign say now?"

I turn. I know just where to look. Over my right shoulder. The stupid ladders. Sign says… "HEAVEN—GO BACK."

There aren't as many bubbles this time.

Imaginary Foes

I knew a unicorn who did not believe in rainbows. He said they were a cruel and subversive plot device to keep the few of us that there are, that's the way he said it, the few of us that there are, from availing ourselves of the pleasures that are here for all, right now.

"I lift my tail to rainbows," he said, and you know what that means, don't you? "I lift my tail to the very idea of rainbows. Both the act and the acted upon being hypothetical," he said with a snort, because we were in a restaurant at the time and tail lifting and it's biological equivalents were to be done outside and only on amenable clouds, so that was primarily on Tuesdays, you see.

"Now, I do like clouds," he said then, breaking into my own thoughts, "clouds are cool, except when they're hot."

I thought the firecrackers we were munching on, such delicious, high density, high decibel crunches they made, were sizzling too brightly in his cerebral cortex. Clouds aren't hot, are they?

"I haven't met any hot clouds, have you?" I asked him. And I must confess I was spraying a little as I spoke. Hot sparks of lightening, that's what firecrackers are, you see, an appetizer of deep fried lightening that has escaped the bolts. Expensive yes, because so hard to collect. Cherubs have cornered that market, so good are they at darting and snatching, and well paid for it too. But, oh the flavor! The fun! Capturing something so amazingly elemental in your fingers, or biological equivalents, and putting, placing or the way I like to do it, tossing it into your mouth, feeling the sweet, spicy spark of it on your tongue, truly an epicurean delight!

"Yes," the unicorn said, "I've met several hot clouds, primarily on Saturdays. They don't like to be bothered on Saturdays, you know, but sometimes, especially if I've eaten lots of stardust, I might not be able to hold it until Tuesday. But still, I like clouds, even the hot angry ones, because they're real, you know, like you and me, not imaginary, like rainbows."

"Oh," I said softly. I lowered my voice, so he would lower his. He was getting a little loud, a little agitated. I watched his tail as it sailed from side to side scattering the fireflies that lit the room. His rhythmless hoof beats made the silverware dance on the table, like I said you eat firecrackers with your hands so we weren't using them. Our drinks, mine a Milky Night and his a Starless Day, puckered and dimpled in their glasses.

The iridescent family at the next table, multi-hued and translucent, turned to stare. Then the father rose from his chair, then the mother, then the eldest son. They arced over my friend the unicorn, casting great swathes of color across his colorless hide.

"Hey" said my friend, "it's the Prisms. Won't you join us?"

But of course, it wasn't the Prisms, it was the Rainbows, but my friend the unicorn never acknowledged that.

Nobody

When a police siren blasted into the stillness of Francine's apartment she woke up. The wail disturbed her soul and gave her goose bumps, her pores contracting and tightening as if to insulate her from loss, because surely a siren meant loss. Of life, freedom, a limb, a future. Somebody would lose something. She shivered and twisted herself up in the three handmade quilts she had gotten from the secondhand store. But she knew she wouldn't be able to go back to sleep. Not without accomplishing something to bring the future closer. Something to chase away the ruthless memories that surfaced every time she heard a siren.

At first it had been fun, and it was fun for a long time. Being away from Mommy. No school. No sneaking out of the house to meet her friends Glorious and Divine—her own party name was Fancy—with clothes her mother wouldn't have let her buy, much less wear, even if she did have the body to carry it off. Now she slept late. Stayed up late, getting into clubs and bars she'd never even heard of. She was fifteen, with fake ID and real designer goods, living it up with Renault on her arm, money in her purse, and nothing but good times on her mind. She'd moved in with Renault, who lived with Bernie and Boy-o. She decorated the three-bedroom apartment and made it more like a home. She cooked and cleaned, putting to use the skills her mother had always insisted on calling a woman's work, but she also shopped and shopped, unlike her mother who did the work of a man and a woman and got no joy or rewards from either. Fancy believed that work was for pay. She'd done the work and the pay was great. Renault always came first, but when he'd become more generous with her, to Bernie and Boy-o, her credit card limits tripled too. And then, after two years of no accidents and no mistakes, she was pregnant.

And then the lock was changed. The credit cards were reported stolen and she was alone.

She'd tried to go home, knowing she'd be made to have an abortion and be forced to live like a child again, but there she was in a three thousand dollar coat with twenty-six dollars and thirty-seven cents in her Kate Spade bag. None of Renault's friends wanted her, would open their doors, answer their phones. When she pushed the buzzer for the third floor walk-up she'd lived in with her mother and two younger brothers an old lady answered. "Shoo. Shoo," she'd told her, this is my apartment now."

Three months later she'd almost lost the baby to hypothermia. February third. Eleven degrees. Three a.m. Blaring sirens. Frozen blood.

They'd told her she'd been comatose for a hundred and forty-three days with no visitors. A cesarean had saved the baby, a girl, and she'd been given up for adoption. Or maybe sent to an orphanage, they weren't sure which. The social worker had gotten married and quit. The sprinklers had gone off in the records room, files drenched, computers fried. Turned out the offsite back-up company was well within their rights to withhold service since they hadn't been paid.

Now sirens gave her chills and spurred her to activity. She got out of bed and crossed her studio apartment to the kitchen area in the dark, stood staring at the glowing twenty-four-inch white stove. Tea? The stove was so clean it looked new. When she'd first invited Joseph to dinner, after a year of coffee shops and movies, he'd examined the garbage, swearing she'd ordered in.

Everything on the kitchen side of the studio was white, except the curtain in front of the tiny window. That was red, a crinkly glittery material that looked like a Slurpy and made her laugh. And cry.

No, no tea. Water.

The room came softly into focus when she turned on the pink lights of the ceiling fixture. The two adjoining walls that defined the bedroom side were turquoise. The third corner, what Joseph called her work-and-play area, was covered with a thickly padded red area rug and scattered with red and turquoise cushions. A chrome gooseneck desk lamp sat on the floor nearby.

Francine went to the closet and pulled out a shoe box for boots. She didn't have the boots, had taken the box from her neighbor's trash, another way she supplemented her income from McDonald's, being an unofficial janitor and errands woman for the other tenants in her building. She took the box to the rug and sat down, irrationally afraid, as always, that she would find nothing inside. Gently she coaxed the contents onto her lap. The child's coat was beautiful, of the softest yellow cashmere she could find. The stitches were so uniform they didn't look like she had sewn them by hand. The dress was almost finished. She smoothed the fabric out on her thighs. Embroidered rainbows scalloped the hem on yellow silk so finely woven and pale it looked like the first light of dawn. Francine hummed as she worked. Not sleepy at all.

🌀 🌀 🌀

Juanita stepped carefully around the limbs of the children sprawled on the playroom floor.

"Mrs. Logan, telephone for you."

Rebecca Logan took the phone without a word and went into the children's room. Five cots and two cribs left a narrow walkway for pacing. She patted her hair lightly, aware that her grey roots were showing, as if the caller could see her. She hoped it was a client and she could unload one of the brats soon, hell, she'd even throw in the cot.

"Hello, Logan Adoptions. This is Mrs. Logan."

There was a jelly stain on her cream-colored blouse and peanut butter under her short blunt fingernails. Sneakers, for Christ's sake, she'd been reduced to wearing sneakers.

"Rebecca? Honey, I need another one," Ralph whispered. His voice was low and hoarse. He'd been smoking, a lot. And probably drinking too. She pictured him hunched over his messy desk in the far corner of the restaurant kitchen, where he could see the menu he planned being created under his exacting glare. His bushy eyebrows would be drawn together over gunmetal grey eyes that constantly circled and searched for something new, something better, something that would take him from struggling entrepreneur to chef of the year. He was probably squeezing that stupid handball in his right hand, keeping his knife hand strong.

"I can't, Ralph. Enough is enough. Somebody's gonna start asking questions."

"Oh, come on!"

She knew he hadn't meant to yell when she heard him suck in a lungful of Marlboro Red.

"Becca, what I mean is, nobody asked before. Remember? And I mean nobody. Don't you get it? Nobody cares."

She heard him self-medicate, more tobacco, some vodka.

"Please, Becky. Please. You want me to beg? All right. I'll beg. I'm begging you. All I need is one more chance and big moneys' in the bag. Stable money. The day after tomorrow. It'd be a corporate account. We'd be their preferred restaurant. Worth well over sixty grand a month. You hear me, Becca? Sixty. I just need to hook them. That's all. Easy. After that I'll work my usual magic. You know me, top of my class, the one to watch, well this time it'll work. I've got the location, the decor, the skills. I can do it. But I need to wow 'em on Thursday. This is the last time. I swear. Please, honey, please." He drew the last words out like a love song, their song.

Rebecca realized she was clenching her jaw so tightly her upper plate was hurting her gums. Her left knee felt a little weak and she began to feel dizzy. The damn little cots were too low to sit on, too hard to get up from. Her doctor said she was overstressed and she'd better retire soon if she wanted the rest of her life to be worth living. But she couldn't afford to retire. Not yet. If she placed three more children this year then maybe. But not before that. With the take on three of the right children she could make the last balloon payment on the condo. With housing expenses taken care of they'd be all right. Not particularly good, but all right. Whether Ralph got this new restaurant, his sixth, off the ground or not.

She turned back toward the door, refusing to deal with Ralph's pleading. She didn't even like talking about it over the phone.

"No, Ralph. No," she said, returning to the playroom, raising her voice. "I gotta go. One of the kids is crying. I gotta go. Bye."

🌀 🌀 🌀

"I asked you before, Joe, don't call me that. Call me Francine."

Those strange horizontal frown lines appeared on her face, and together with the faint pimple scars that were perfectly lined up above her brows they reminded Joseph of the tiny perforation holes used to tear and separate paper.

"That's how you introduced yourself to me," he said. "That's all I've ever called you. You couldn't stand the name Francine. What's the big deal?"

He looked over the stained and pitted coffee cup that was halfway to his mouth and willed the truth from her. He didn't think she actually lied to him, but she sure could keep a secret.

"So what? That was then. Back then when I didn't want you to get too close. I gave you my street name, my nickname, but now, well, now we're close, and I want you to think of me as the person I am, not the person I was."

"But I didn't know the person you were. I only know who you are now. And I know you as Fancy and I love you as Fancy. Francine is just a name to me."

"Well, if it's just a name then you'll get used to it."

"But why should I have to?"

"Look, Joe. That was then. This is me now. In the near future I'm not gonna have to ask nobody if they 'wanna super-size that,' or if they 'want an apple pie.' I won't have to give a damn if it's for here or to go. I ain't gotta say 'there ain't no bathroom,' or 'we don't have a public restroom,' either. I won't have to say 'theater three, second door on the left' no damn more!"

She took a breath, dramatically, as if swinging into her next act, "I'll be saying stuff like, 'Good morning, my name is Francine Foote, and I'm here to wire your computer network. Where do you want the servers?' Fancy sounds like a stripper's name. Now how would I look, especially built like I am, all breasts and hips, saying 'Hi, my name is Fancy, and I'ma get down on my hands and knees and crawl around under your desks?' Huh? Which sounds better? More professional? I can't be calling myself Fancy no more. They gonna doubt me anyway because I'm Black. And a woman. Fancy Foote? Uh-uh. I need to be taken seriously."

"You mean Willoughby, don't you?" He threw the question out casually, hoping for a serious answer. That would make eight, or was it eighty proposals? He'd first asked her to marry him five months after they'd met at an electronics supply store. He'd been checking out digital cameras, teasing his hobby of photography, and she'd watched him so intensely that he shifted his attention from the salesclerk to her.

"Do I know you?" he'd asked.

That was the first time he'd seen that frown.

"Well, then, do you think you know me? What're you looking at? Why're you watching me?"

"I'm wondering what you're gonna use that for, specifically."

He could tell she was really expecting an answer.

She didn't look crazy. And even though she wasn't the prettiest woman in the store she looked really good in her black skirt and tight blue sweater. But Joseph hadn't bothered to answer, just turned away and continued grilling the salesman.

The woman had sucked her teeth, slow and loud, but hadn't moved away, except to shift from one foot to the other, advancing a couple of inches closer.

When Joseph left the store with his camera under his arm, his thoughts returned to the woman with the plushy looking breasts and the big teeth. Why'd she think she could just stare him down like that? Half a block later he decided to ask her. He went back and found her at the cashier.

"What so interested you," he started when he was within shouting distance, "that you had to stand around and watch me buy a camera?"

Francine had looked at him and nodded, counting out $7.98 in singles, dimes, and pennies. He looked like the men she was familiar with, in jeans and an oversized Knicks jersey, but his hair was all wrong, barber shop neat, lined edges, and he needed his eyeglasses, they weren't sunglasses for style, even though they'd shaded to a dark green.

"You. Your questions were so detailed that I figured I could learn something if I just took the time."

She'd closed her change purse with a loud snap and buried it deep in a big backpack. She'd smiled and said thank-you to the cashier, but when she turned back to him her smile was gone.

"What interested you so much you had to come back and ask me?"

She'd started out the door and he'd followed. And even after three years Joseph still didn't understand all of what Fancy really wanted. Why she worked so hard but never seemed to have any money or now, why she was moving from her studio to a two-bedroom apartment, without him.

"I'm not ready to get married just yet, Joe." She reached across the table and pinched his cheek, as if he were a child to be lured through the grocery store with promises of candy at the checkout.

"I told you. I have something to do first." She said this lightly, cheerfully, as she always did. Her wide mouth spread a good two inches wider as she gave him that lips-closed smile that was as good as a locked door. It was part of Fancy's nature to keep setting goals and that was fine, one of the things he liked about her, but when was she going to trust him enough to tell him about them?

When Lashaila woke up to go to the bathroom it was dark and quiet. Well, maybe not so dark. If she turned her head she could see the red glow of the sign on the wall over the door, by Kim's bed. And maybe it wasn't so quiet either. She could hear the sounds from the outside. That was a car. And that, a bus. And that was a truck and some more cars. Talking and yelling and gun shots from Juanita's TV, too. She liked the shows that were loud and then soft, something scary happened and then a lot of people talked about it. The scary parts had woken her up before.

Lashaila sat up and pushed her short chubby legs off the bed and slid down to the floor on the side away from the door. That was important. She was glad she remembered. Mrs. Logan talked about going the extra mile, and that meant if she did everything the long way, her wish would come true. She put on her new slippers, which were more fuzzy pink tops than squishy white bottoms.

Mrs. Logan had given them to her yesterday when she gave stuff to everybody from a big black plastic bag Miss Juanita found by the door. The slippers were too big, but Mrs. Logan said that didn't matter, she should wear them anyway.

Lashaila walked slowly between the rows of cots, picking up and putting down each foot carefully, trying to control the slippers so she wouldn't make too much noise. Juanita didn't like noise. Maria rolled over and grabbed for her doll, Mush-Mush. Mush-Mush was on the floor. Lashaila picked Mush-Mush up and put her back against Maria's chest. Maria's arms and legs curled around her doll. Maria was only two years old and she needed Mush-Mush. When Lashaila was little she slept with her doll too. But now she was a big girl, and Mommy-Baby lived on the shelf over her bed. She only came down when Lashaila really needed her. Lashaila hadn't slept with MommyBaby at all since she started waking up to go to the bathroom, and MommyBaby looked kind of lonely, on the shelf with only her picture of a house with two windows to keep her company. But before that, when she was little, she had slept with MommyBaby every night and never let her fall on the floor. When a real Mommy Lady came and picked her, then she and the real Mommy Lady and MommyBaby would go live in a house with two windows. Lamar went. And so did Qiana and Marshawn and Kelvin. Soon it would be her turn too. When a real Mommy Lady picked her.

"Good night, children. See you tomorrow."

"See you tomolow!" yelled Ashley, abandoning her alphabet puzzle to throw herself towards Mrs. Logan's knees. Her two blond ponytails and startlingly blue eyes making her look just like the doll she thrust up at Rebecca Logan. "Kiss good-bye. Kiss good-bye."

"Oh, I almost forgot, didn't I? But you know I'd never forget you, Ashley. I'd get all the way to the car and turn right back. Just to give you and Baby Cathy a kiss."

Mrs. Logan bent down and put her arms around eighteen-month-old Ashley. "First, a big hug," she said, and Ashley's stubby little arms tried to encircle Mrs. Logan's head.

"She still can't get that hugging thing down to the right level," said Juanita as she moved around the room, picking up toys and straightening the miniature tables and chairs. Rebecca knew when she got back tomorrow morning that the children would all have been fed, bathed, and put to bed with little disobedience and no tears. The children were getting used to Juanita, and Rebecca was glad to have found her. She was a lot cheaper than Darla, but wasn't as motherly. Darla had been with her for years, but recently she'd started asking a lot of questions and bugging her for a raise in pay. Juanita was a little nosy though, and Rebecca had started locking the file cabinet, something she hadn't done for years.

"But isn't she precious? She's just the cutest thing here!" Mrs. Logan gave Ashley a long noisy kiss.

"Now, Catti. Catti." Ashley pushed Baby Cathy at Rebecca's face, knocking her glasses around toward her ears.

"Easy, Ashley," Juanita cautioned, "be gentle."

"Oh, it's all right. Leave her alone, Juanita. She's so sweet. Aren't you just the sweetest little angel? Okay, there's a big kiss for Baby Cathy. I'll see you tomorrow."

Rebecca adjusted her glasses and struggled to stand up.

"See you tomolow!" Ashley yelled at her again.

"Yes, bye-bye, sweetie. And Juanita, take what's left of the turkey off the bone so they can have turkey sandwiches for lunch tomorrow."

"Yuck, turkey." Justin was on the floor in front of the TV, rolling a Hess oil tanker between his thin brown thighs.

"Justin sure doesn't like turkey." Juanita said. She was not looking forward to getting him to eat his dinner again tonight.

"No, but who cares? It's that or nothing for him. Have a good night. Oh, and I have a nine thirty appointment with Ashley tomorrow, so make sure she's in a good mood."

She heard the door being locked and bolted behind her as she went down the steps, knees groaning in protest. She shouldn't have squatted like that to hug Ashley, but lifting her up was difficult too. I'm getting too old for this, she thought. But tomorrow could be my lucky day. If that nice couple from East 63rd Street wanted Ashley, and she was sure they would, she'd be up forty thousand dollars. But Justin. And the others. They were a problem. At best she'd clear maybe seven or eight thou for each. If she could move them. But nobody wanted black children. And she just couldn't make enough off of them when she did find a taker. They just sat around taking up space. It took two or three Ashleys to support the rest of the little black bastards. But what could she do? She couldn't say no. When her agency name came up on the list she had to take whatever child was next.

With Ashley gone, she'd concentrate on Maria. She wasn't really white, but she had very, very light skin and her hair wasn't that curly. Oh, who was she kidding? It was curly and would only get worse. I'll have to get Juanita to give her a reverse perm. Darla did one on Isabella and it came out beautifully. Although she'd said it'd grow out curly again, but by then the brat was gone and the check had cleared. Maybe I'll change Maria's name. Give her something with a little more dignity, like Elisabeth or Sarah. She's too young to know she's Puerto Rican. And I'm too old to keep this up much longer.

⑨ ⑨ ⑨

"Where have you been? Just where the hell have you been, Rebecca? I've been waiting for you for over half an hour!"

Ralph was sitting at the kitchen table, in the dark. Rebecca saw the glowing tip of his cigarette suspended near where his mouth would be. She imagined the bottle of vodka beside him. And the cut crystal glass from the set her mother gave them balancing precariously on his knee. Why couldn't he just use a regular glass? And put it on the table?

"I'm not late, Ralph. This is the time I always get home on my early nights. You know that." She thought about leaving the door open. Leaving her pocketbook on her shoulder.

The kitchen table had seen better days. It, and the six chairs, now reduced to three, had been a smooth-as-glass mahogany dining room set when they'd bought it twenty years ago. But after being shunted around almost yearly for the first fifteen years, the table was scarred and scratched and didn't stand as firmly as it had before.

"Whaddya mean, I know that? Don't try to tell me what I know. You think you're so much better than me. And don't you ever, ever hang up on me again."

He got up just as she turned on the light and was disoriented by the glare. Thick dark hair fell over his forehead.

71

She liked it at this stage best, right before he'd get a haircut, a little long, the strands of grey documenting his adventures, echoing his eyes. He was slim and fit, yet the suit that she was still paying for was creased in all the wrong places. Tomorrow she'd take it to the cleaners.

"Ralph, I was just saying, it's about six thirty now; usually you're at the restaurant at this time of the evening. How'd it go today?" She eased herself down on the soft, but not quite saggy, faded blue couch, and put her feet up on the coffee table, watching, fascinated, as the crevices of angry tension on Ralph's face seemed to evaporate.

"Hey, Becky, yeah. Look, I'm sorry. I'm just all keyed up and a little on edge is all." He rushed to sit close to her, throwing a pillow to the floor so he could snuggle his right arm around her shoulders. He cradled the glass of vodka in his left hand and began rolling it around on her cheek.

Not Ashley, she thought. Not Ashley. I know he'll want her. She's the plumpest. But I'm not willing to make a forty thousand dollar investment in that place. He'd be doing me a favor if he took that damn Justin. But he won't want him. Too old. Too skinny. But I've got to keep Ashley. And I'd better hold onto Maria, too. That leaves Lashaila, she's young enough, still has her baby fat. There's Rueben too. I always forget about him, he's so quiet, he's not too big. Not too skinny. Ralph'll say the others are too old, I'm sure. So that's it then. Lashaila or Rueben. Whichever, I don't care, so long as it's not Ashley. Or Maria.

Rebecca pulled away some so she could look her husband in the eyes. Ready.

"Look, honey. I need a child. Tonight," his voice was steady, although his hand trembled on the back of her neck.

"No."

He traced a slow circle at the pulse point just under her ear. Right where he knew his kiss touched her heart.

"No, I said." She breathed deeply and regularly, putting her two meditation classes to use, trying to control her stress. "I have a business too, Ralph, and you're cutting into my profit."

"What profit? I'm reducing your liabilities, you mean. You ought to thank me." He tried a small smile, but her eyes wouldn't let him enlarge on it. "Look, honey, when the restaurant takes off, you can close shop," he said, bringing the vodka to her lips, offering her a sip. "I know you're not feeling so good these days."

Her lips parted involuntarily. Accepting.

"Besides, you don't make that much anyway."

Again he tried a smile, but his words burned like rotgut.

"I've made enough to support us both for the last ten years," she said quietly.

She supposed it was the Catholic in her that made her start the negotiations this way. She'd given up four kids in nine months and had found that pain was a quicker release than penance.

She couldn't blame him. Or she couldn't blame him alone. It was she who let five-month-old Lamar slip under the bath water and drown when Ashley fell down and hit her head. It was she who panicked and bundled Lamar's dead body and took it home with her, telling Darla that he'd been picked up for a test weekend with prospective parents. And it was she, Rebecca Logan, of

Logan's Adoption Agency who calmed down when she realized in a very personal and profound way that nobody cared about a dead black boy. Calmly and skillfully, with Ralph's cleaver, she butchered Lamar and put the meat in the freezer. She threw out the pieces one at a time, along with the vegetable parings and empty toilet paper rolls that made up the rest of the garbage. But she came home one evening and found Ralph eating roasted slices of thigh. And loving it. So she couldn't blame him, alone.

She braced herself for the pain as the glass smashed into her forehead, sloshing vodka onto her scalp. She imagined it numbing her brain as his fingers tightened on the back of her neck. Vodka dripped down her glasses like artificial tears. He dropped the unbroken glass in her lap and used the thumb side of his fist to punch her below her breasts, between the ribs. He had perfect aim and perfect execution. The air rushed from her lungs, muscles too shocked and weakened to draw breath before the next blow came. And the next. Her heart sputtered. Blood pounded on both sides of the locked gate of his hand around the back of her neck.

But absolution didn't take nearly as long as it used to.

She shoved the coffee table away with her feet and twisted her upper body around enough to grab his crotch and squeeze his balls.

"Let's not fight," she mouthed and hissed and croaked, maintaining the pressure on his testicles, watching him resist the urge to wrench himself away.

"Let's not," he agreed.

As Francine got off the bus in front of the Social Services Child Welfare Division building, she saw Malik flip his cigarette into the street and stroll back to his post by the door. The shattered glass was still held in place with packing tape, and she wondered if they'd ever get the door fixed. It looked like it had been hit by a bullet, but it was only Angelique. Angelique's six-year-old daughter had decided to take her three-year-old sister to the bathroom in Macy's. Angelique found Macy's Security and Security found the girls, but instead of returning the girls to her, Angelique had been arrested and charged with negligence. Her daughters were driven off somewhere in a government car while her hands were handcuffed behind her back. Malik had been able to usher Angelique and her husband out of the Social Services office, but when Angelique's husband went to get their car, Angelique had attacked the door with her shoe. Some shoe. What kind of shoe could do that, Francine always wondered, though she knew it wasn't the shoe, but the mother wielding it.

"Hey, Francine, what're you doing back here so soon?" Malik opened the door for her, "Weren't you just here on Tuesday?"

"Hey, Malik. Getting close, Malik, getting close."

"They found your baby yet?"

"If they had, I'da been floating in here on a cloud, but I got to stay on her, you know."

"It's a damn shame, Francine, a damn shame," he said. His consolation to almost everyone.

After two hours Francine's caseworker, Irene Harris, looked exactly as she had on any number of previous visits. Hair more salt than pepper pulled back tight and supplemented with a stick-on bun. Her skin was smooth and wrinkle free. No make-up. No glasses. No smile. Grey suit with the grey blouse with the pearl buttons. Francine felt like she knew the woman's entire wardrobe.

"Francine, I told you I'd call you if I found out anything." Irene got up and went to the door of her tiny office, ready to signal in the next problem.

"But you didn't call me." Francine walked over to the front of the battered black metal desk, her solid heeled pumps thumping up dust on the well-worn path through the industrial carpet. She sat down and crossed her legs. Then uncrossing them, she leaned forward, trying to look for her name among the files neatly piled up on Irene's desk. The pile was almost a foot high.

Irene sighed loudly and went back to the side of her desk that was farthest away from Francine and stood with her arms crossed.

"These things take time," she said, "I can't just work a miracle because you want one."

The swish of her stockings on her thighs was the only noise in their little space as Francine put her pocketbook on the floor and crossed her legs again. She thought they both looked like they were on their way to church. She was wearing her grey suit too.

"But Ms. Harris, it shouldn't take a miracle to know where a child in your system is," she said, trying to sound as if this were an impersonal conversation. Something you talk about after reading the newspaper. "You all are supposed to be keeping track of children, looking after them and making sure they're being treated right. You have to know where they are in order to do that."

"You know your case has extenuating circumstances," Irene said, smiling.

"But you've known about my 'extenuating circumstances' for almost two years now. I know you're busy, but I'm one of your cases too."

"It's not that I'm not working on it, Fancy."

"Please call me Francine," Fancy said wondering why she hadn't told the woman to call her Ms. Foote. *Ms. Harris knows too much about me, maybe too much.*

"It's not that I'm not working on it, Francine. I am. I just saw you the other day. It's just that, it's just that I don't have any answers for you today."

"Well, why not? What exactly is the problem? What's the last thing that you found out?"

Irene looked across the tops of the six filing cabinets that lined the left wall like sentinels and stared at the pictures of her husband, her parents, her children, her Lord.

"I told you, there are thirteen four-year-old girls spread out all over the city who could be your daughter. We're trying to find out which one."

Francine knew what Ms. Harris was looking at. Had seen her scan those pictures a hundred times.

"That's what you've been telling me. What I want to know is how? How are you trying to find out? What are you doing? Now?"

Voices rose in the waiting room, as loud as an explosion.

Irene, waiting for the noise to recede to normal disgruntlement, picked up a stack of mail and opened the first letter. She took the letter out, unfolded it, and put it on the desk. She reached under her desk and threw the envelope away. Then she took up the second envelope. She looked at Francine and smiled. Opened the envelope. Took out the letter. Unfolded it and laid it on top of the first one.

Francine watched her open her mail without reading the contents. She swung her foot restlessly, but her upper body was still. She looked around at the dingy green walls and the dusty hanging plant that never grew because it was plastic.

When it was as quiet as could be reasonably expected Irene began, "Listen, Francine, I know it seems like we've been working on this for a long time, and I can assure you that we're doing everything we can—"

"No. I've been working." Francine's hands were on her hips before she was out of the chair. "I'm the one who's been working. When I first met you, you told me I couldn't take care of my daughter if I had her. Well, now I can. I've been working my ass off, going to school and working two piece-of-shit jobs and saving money. I graduated from CNE school yesterday, do you remember that? This weekend I'm moving into a two-bedroom apartment. Couple of weeks after that I start my new job. I've given you proof of every damn thing you've ever asked me for. So don't come at me with 'we've been working' because you ain't told me nothing new in seventeen months."

Irene repositioned her standard issue chair with the handmade needlepoint cushion and sat down. The chair squeaked, accepting her weight. Francine sat back down. They stared at each other, listening to screams of "I didn't do it! I didn't do it!" coming from a woman down the hall. A baby in the waiting room started crying. They heard Malik running toward the screams.

"Ms. Harris, what have you done, since Tuesday, to find out where my daughter is?"

Irene picked up her pen.

"Well, what's the next step then? Shit, give me the list and I'll go see the little girls."

"You know I can't do that. Besides, what good would that do, you don't even know what she looks like, not even what she could look like, not knowing who the father is."

Fancy wanted to jump up on the desk and kick Ms. Harris right in the face, see that bun going flying off into the corner. She wanted to go through all the files and find the list of little girls and take them all home with her. She wanted to shake the whole city upside down until her baby landed in her lap. She wanted to cry.

She took a deep breath and let it out loudly. "Okay, you got your dig in."

"I didn't mean—"

"Yes, you did. But let's move on. So what would the next step be?" Her voice was calm, but her feet tapped noiselessly on the brown plaid carpet.

"We'd have to get an Order for DNA testing signed by the Family Court Judge, but I don't think—"

"Call somebody!" Fancy shouted, once more on her feet, leaning over the desk. She picked up the telephone receiver and threw it at Irene's pearl buttons. "Call somebody right now! Do your damn job! Now!"

Fancy realized she was yelling. Yelling at the woman whose help she needed, tried to lower her voice, saw her fists coming down on the desk as the receiver bounced around on its curled cord. She felt the pain, but still she pounded. "Help me, goddamn you! Help me! Find my daughter!"

By the time Malik got there she was crying. He picked up her pocketbook and put the strap on her shoulder, ushering her out.

◈ ◈ ◈

"Reservations for Willoughby."

"Ahh, yes, right this way, sir, madam."

"This is a nice place, Joe, have you been here before?" Francine trailed behind Joe and the maitre d', trying to take in the softly lit wall sconces, thick white carpeting, and dozens of waiters scurrying around with linen towels over the arms. The maitre d' held out the red velvet cushioned chair for her, and she concentrated on positioning her butt just right. Once she was settled she found Joe watching her, smiling. She repeated the question.

"No, not exactly," he hedged. "This place is under new management. The chef is now the owner, and I figure that's always good. I heard the guys at work talking about it. It's supposed to be really great." He paused and shook his right arm from the shoulder down, like a boxer loosening up. "And I wanted tonight to be special."

"Oh, yeah? And why is that?" Francine tried to keep her tone light. She reached across the table and pulled his fingers apart, which were entwined with one another as if in prayer. She put them on the table gently, backs down, and placed her palms over his fingers, his fingers on her palms. He looked at her and smiled, slid his hands out and onto his lap.

"I brought you here to celebrate your graduation. Congratulations, again. I'm very proud of you, Fancy, uh, Francine."

"Thanks, Joe. That means a lot to me. You know, that you're proud of me, Mr. Degreed Up Account Manager."

Joe let that pass, knowing how sensitive Francine was about her missteps on the way to maturity.

"I also brought you here because I want you to remember tonight."

Francine wanted to laugh, wanted to stay with the feelings of accomplishment and pride and celebration. Her foot began to dance under the table, but just as quickly stopped. Joe's eyes, deep set and wide apart, shielded behind his unfashionable glasses, looked worried, the shallow tracks outlining his mouth smoothed out slightly, as they did when he was trying to make the best of something he didn't really like.

"Francine, I need an answer from you. Tonight. I don't want to keep hanging around if you're not going to marry me."

She could see it hurt him to say it. Even though he'd said the words quickly, like he'd rehearsed them a thousand times, they still had a visible impact on him. She watched him retreat into his own deeply cushioned chair.

The waiter appeared and presented their menus. They studied them in silence, glancing up at each other with the tentative smiles of new friends as their water glasses were filled.

"Our specials tonight are the young and tender offerings of spring. We offer a spring garden salad, yes, of baby spinach, fennel and arugula, with lightly toasted sesame seeds, drizzled with a delicate lemon vinaigrette. Yes, and after that we suggest our own, homemade right here, today, wild mushroom ravioli with our very special olive oil. You may wish to accompany that with our grilled tuna steak in white wine and dill sauce. Or if you prefer, our most amazing lamb medallions, that the chef has just perfected, unlike any lamb you've had before, so tender and flavorful they are accented only with subtle hints of thyme."

"What do you think, Francine? Either of those sound good to you?"

"Yes, the lamb sounds very good. I love lamb."

"Yes, very good. And you, sir?"

"Ah, I'll have the grilled tuna, please."

"Very well, sir."

As the waiter left they both reached for their water.

Francine took a sip. And then another. Then she studied the tablecloth for as long as she could while Joe sat in silence.

"I do want to marry you, Joe," she said. "But there's something you have to know first. Over dessert, okay? We are having dessert, aren't we? This is such a great place, let's just enjoy the food first."

"Oh, so you're finally going to tell me, huh?"

"Tell you what?"

"I don't know. Whatever. I know you've got some kind of secret. Something that drives you."

Francine looked away. She looked at the couple at the table nearest to them. The big blond woman sat with her back ramrod straight, as if she expected to be photographed at any minute. The man's tie was knotted so tightly that his neck bulged out over his collar. She looked at the waiters, noticing that they were all short and white, with dark hair, and the busboys, men really, were even shorter, with darker skin and darker hair. When she let her gaze flit across Joseph's face again she saw that he'd let it go, for now.

The lamb medallions were delicious, as promised, better than any lamb she'd ever tasted. So this is what the rich people eat, she joked, but in the calm slow blinking of Joe's eyes she saw the relentless ticking of his clock.

After desserts of chocolate mousse for Joe and passion fruit sorbet for her Francine took several deep breaths, trying to prepare herself. She twirled a miniature goblet of brandy around by its stem. She felt even more upset than she'd anticipated. She'd told herself, over and over, that it wasn't important. If Joseph rejected her because of her daughter then so be it. But her heart was beating too fast, and her stomach was beginning to hurt. Pin-pricks of perspiration made her dress irritate her back, her thighs. She could feel sweat forming on her scalp and wished she could bury both hands in her hair and get a good scratch going, but she could almost feel her mother's glare. Mommy had not allowed any hair touching at the table.

Her breathing became shallower, and she forced the words through the tightening noose in her throat, her words no more than a whisper. Joseph leaned forward, straining to hear without interrupting, giving her his full attention while she told him what he most wanted to know. She was a mother, working to reclaim her child. Lashaila—that's what someone, God only knew who, had named her baby girl—had been shifted around so often that the state had lost track of her. She was *this close* to finding out where she actually was.

"To be honest," Joe said, "I thought it was something like that."

"What? You did?"

"C'mon, Francine. I'm not stupid. I see the way you look at children. I've also noticed that you never, ever talk about them. I figured either you had a child, somewhere, or that something bad had happened to a child of yours, or else—"

"Or else what?" Although *what* didn't seem to matter anymore because Joseph hadn't gotten up and walked out, even though he was too much of a gentleman to do that. In smaller actions, his eyes would have closed somewhat, shutting out what he didn't want to dwell on and he would have narrowed his beautiful expressive nostrils, breathing in short bursts. Instead, he was just talking, calmly, as he had on countless other nights, picking up a subject, a problem, examining it from all sides, proposing a solution, an alternative, a possibility.

"Or else you knew that you couldn't have children and so you were working hard to make a career for yourself, you know, be a career woman. But that would have been okay, too. I mean we would've worked it out. Just like this, like your daughter, Lashaila. We'll work it out. Stop looking so worried. We'll work it out. I love you."

"Oh," was all she could manage. She hadn't really heard his answer, was just watching his lips move, thinking how much she loved him, how much she hadn't wanted to lose him, his love, his respect. Was that why her insides were quaking?

"Why didn't you tell me before? You didn't trust me?"

"I didn't trust—" was all she could get out before rushing to the ladies' room, bile rising in her throat.

Birdbrain

I hate birds. Every time something bad happens or is about to happen, there's a goddamn bird somewhere around.

The day I met my father he brought me a parakeet. Why he thought a twelve-year-old girl would want a parakeet, I don't know. I guess I didn't like birds even then. I know he was trying to be nice. When I feel generous I tell myself that he was giving me a living emblem of his love or some such bullshit. Other times I think he was putting a mojo on me. And Mommy. Since it turned out that she was so allergic to the damn thing that we had to get rid of it. Which was just as well, because I was either gonna let it starve or fatten it up and serve it to him when he came back. That's if I could have kept it alive for another twelve years.

As it turns out.

The next time I actually saw the man I was twenty-four. Damn if he didn't come to my door at seven in the morning. The news was blaring about some rare missing bird and the twelve thousand dollar reward for its return. And here he comes, asking me to lend him a hundred and twenty-seven fifty. Just goes to show how out of touch with reality he was. Still, it pissed me off so bad that I went to the firing range and shot me up a whole lot of fake birds. In the heart. In the eye. In the wing. I even shot one in the foot and got him again in the other foot before he hit the ground. And you know how big a bird foot is.

So now it's another twelve years later, and I'm strolling to work in my new red suit, swinging my pocketbook and smiling at the other wage slaves. I look a lot like a carnation, all round and dimply, but I feel like a rose. Then there's this plop on my left breast, and I look down at pigeon shit.

I want to go home. No, I *want* to go to Tahiti. But, I go on. I just keep walking and go inside the medical billing office where I'm a cog in the healthcare wheel that pretends to be about prolonging our lives, instead of more accurately timing our deaths. I try not to think about it, because you, know, I like to eat. So I pretend that Mother Nature has pinned me with the first brooch of spring. Never mind that it's August twelfth and ninety-six degrees. My fault for being in a damn red suit anyway, right? Trying to look cute and competent on my j-o-b like my mother taught me. I'm so *not mad* I get perverse. Don't even wipe it off. Every time somebody points it out to me I rush to the bathroom and then come back with the shit still intact.

Finally my supervisor tells me, point blank, to go home and change.

So sure, I'll go home, but I ain't coming back.

I don't want to waste fifty-five minutes of my newly freed time slugging through subway tunnels and climbing on buses, so I decide to take a taxi home. Of course, it takes me, a Black woman on Broadway and 56th Street headed uptown in New York City, suit or no damn suit, damn near twenty minutes to catch a taxi. I'm la-di-da-ing it though. Feeling really proud of myself for not giving in to stress. It ain't what happens, it's how you handle it and all that.

When I get home, before I even turn on the light, I smell my mother's perfume. It's a kind of light breezy smell, as if she's free, white, and twenty-one. I remember when our perfume of choice was Dial Spring Breeze or Secret Powder Fresh. I turn on the light and there she is. Sitting on my white leather couch in her own red suit, except hers has a waist. She's got a bottle of gin between her legs, a glass in her left hand, and a tissue that looked better in the box in her right.

"Mommy! What's wrong? What's the matter?" I drop my pocketbook and go running over.

My mother looks up at me with such hope and trust that I pray to God I can make whatever it is all right. Her eyes pool over and fresh tears cruise down her pretty face.

"What? What? Tell me." Her hands are cool. As if she's been sitting here too long and is numb. Her back shudders with the convulsions of trying to hold back tears, trying for control. Petite and cute as my mother is, she is not a dainty crier. She looks at me and opens her mouth to speak, but instead it sounds as if the church balcony has collapsed and the choir is falling on the congregation.

I climb on my knees on the couch and wrap my arms around her, cradling her head to my breast. Not *that* breast, the other breast. Finally I can make out a couple of words.

He's dead.

Relief overpowers me, and I fall back on the snotty tissues. He who? Ain't no he I know that's worth all this.

Don't get me wrong, I've had some good men. Key word being *had*. They seem to like me fine, until I start using bad grammar, like we's our'n, and us'n.

My mother shifts in mid-wail, down two or three octaves, from grief right into anger, and pushes me away. Immediately I feel guilty for not being as upset as she is.

"Don't you read the papers?" she yells at me, swatting at me with her free hand.

"Ma, what happened? Who are you talking about? Is Frank all right?"

Frank is the only man I can think of who might be able to reduce my mother to tears. She's never been serious about a man before, but I didn't think he was quite this important. She'd been seeing him for two months, and so far I knew he had a great job, a great smile, and could make grocery shopping an adventure.

"It's your father! Your father! It's all in the paper. He's dead. And he blamed it on me!"

"That son of a bitch!"

She punches me on the thigh, a lot harder this time. I don't curse in front of my mother, and talking bad about my father was never allowed. It just slipped out. I bent down to retrieve the newspaper at her feet. It was open to an article about a bank robbery. Either that or a yachting accident on the Long Island Sound.

Apparently my father, Rupert James, had walked into a bank in the diamond district with two toy guns strapped to a holster under his jacket. A holster! He'd waited on line and then politely asked the teller for four hundred thousand dollars in hundreds, twenties, and tens. She asked him to fill out a withdrawal slip. Enter the guns.

The security guard shot him in the back of the neck. No arrest, no trial, no questions, fast forward straight to the execution.

He was carrying a suicide note addressed to Tillie. My mother, Matilda Lancaster.

Mom had pretty much stopped crying and was glaring at me by the time I finished the article. I threw the paper back on the floor and went to get myself a glass. Mom was right, this definitely called for gin, a ladies drink.

I didn't say anything. Couldn't say anything civil. Just sat down and held her hand until she shook me off.

"You didn't know him like I did," she said.

My mother would understate the apocalypse. When I was little and we ate beans and franks in candlelight for six months she told me our chicken was on lay-away. So no, I didn't know him like she did. First of all, I was his daughter, not his would-be-common-law-but-they-didn't-live-together-long-enough-wife. Second of all, I'd only seen him four or five times in thirty-six years. I had spoken to him on the phone at least a dozen times though. He'd call me late at night, particularly on Halloween and Father's Day, when he was drunk. I didn't really dislike the man, he just wasn't within my sights.

"Don't you feel *anything*? He was your father!"

She looks at me like I'm in need of sensitivity training.

"Why'd he do it, you think?" I ask, as gently as I can, muffling my words in my drink.

Her long red nails begin clicking against her empty glass, as if counting off the obvious reasons a Black man would need four hundred thousand dollars in small bills.

"He did it because he loved us," she says.

Bullshit, is what I'm thinking, but I bring my glass up to my lips so fast I almost chip my teeth. Maybe that's why I'm a little round in some places. I put stuff in my mouth to keep other stuff from coming out. I can't look at her though. I'm trying hard not to laugh. I just keep swallowing gin. It gives me time to think.

Now, my Grandmother didn't raise no fool. But neither did my mother, so *I* must've missed something here. Like maybe the past thirty-something years?

"Ma, when was the last time you saw him?" I ask.

This time my mother hides her words in her drink. Twickslo, it sounds like.

"What? Say that again please?" It didn't sound like *I ain't seen that dog since the devil was in short pants* to me.

She sighs, a long sigh, like a woman with an affliction she'd long since learned to live with.

"The last time I saw him was two weeks ago," she says and takes a deep breath, "but I never stopped seeing him. When I saw him two weeks ago I told him I couldn't see him anymore."

I choke on the gin, and it goes up my sinuses and sets my brain on fire.

"What? You've been having an affair with my own father? Behind my back? Without even telling me? How long has this been going on?" I jump up from the couch and go into full Johnnie Cochran mode.

"Where'd you see him? Two weeks ago? Did he come to your house? Did you go to his? Does he even have a house?" I pace back and forth in front of her. Kick off my shoes. Almost lose my balance. Guess I'm a little drunk.

My mother looks at me with eyes as dull as marbles, looking every bit the hostile witness. I imagine the judge on my right, perched in the entertainment center, near the door, so he can make a quick getaway. The jury is already coming out of deliberation from my bedroom on the left. Ma takes a sip of her drink and rolls her eyes.

"Don't start with me, Marva." She reaches down to pick up the newspaper and tears the page with the article away from the others. I stand there, staring at her with my mouth hanging open for so long that I can feel my spit turning to drool. The room begins to sway but I refuse to sit down.

"What's that mess on your jacket?" she asks.

"Huh?"

"Look," Ma starts, waiting until I seem to be focusing on her, "I enjoyed your father, but he was not the kind of man I wanted you to grow up around."

"Huh?"

"I loved him, all right?! He was smart and funny and charming. Fun. Plus I could always count on him to um…you know, stroke my feathers, keep my pressure down." She pats her thigh, re-crosses her legs. "But he had a low tolerance for working. He said he didn't want to shore up the power system that he felt should be dismantled, didn't want to work within it, you know, putting up with all the stuff that gets the rent paid and food on the table. He was a theoretical revolutionary, but he didn't have the stomach for doing the real work. He wasn't good at family things either, like birthdays or dance lessons or funerals." She looks at me as if I'm deliberately trying to be dense.

I sit down. Right on the floor, eye level with my mother's feet, which are now propped up on the coffee table.

"So, what, Ma? You're telling me that you've been seeing my father all along? All my life? That y'all had a relationship and I wasn't included?" My mother seems to be sitting at both ends of the couch at once because my eyes keep crossing. And it seems to me that there are two of her. One I thought I knew and one I didn't know at all. How could she have kept so much from me for so long? Or was I so blind, that I just never noticed?

"I know this is hard for you to understand, but I did it for your own good." She leans forward and from where I sit her head seems to rise up outta her knees.

"*You* did it? *You* kept my father away from me? Is that what you did? For my own good?" I can feel my throat starting to close up, like I'm gonna cry. But I refuse to cry. I refuse. Because I would not be crying for my father, the damn fool, I'd be crying for myself.

"Marva, listen, he didn't want to do any of the things that I needed done. He wasn't gonna check your homework or make sure you ate dinner while I ironed clothes—"

"Well, what about the movies? He could have taken me to the movies couldn't he? Fun stuff like that?"

"He was broke! Aren't you listening to me? He robbed a bank, for Christ's sake!"

"He never had any money? Not ever? Not even once, that he could buy me an ice cream? He couldn'ta sat down and taught me basketball rules, so I don't call a foul a strike? He shoulda been there to give Darnell the evil eye when I went out on my first date! Remember that? Although you did look pretty scary when you answered the door with a baseball bat and a cigarette behind your ear."

"Yeah, that was good, wasn't it? What ever happened to Darnell?"

"On Monday he told everybody that you were a butch and I was a lesbo in training because I wouldn't let him up under my skirt." I reach for the bottle of gin and pour myself another shot.

"Oh, honey, I'm sorry." She leans back and stares up at the ceiling. There are salty tear marks under her chin and lines on her neck that I never noticed before.

"I'm sorry. Why didn't you tell me?" she asks.

"What was the point? I knew you were doing the best you could. But now I find out that I really did have a father."

"That's what I'm trying to tell you," she says, still looking at the ceiling, "just because I saw the man regularly did not mean that you had a father. He didn't want to be a father. Or a husband either."

"But why? Why? Why not?"

Mommy slams her feet down on the floor and rocks forward with the speed of a somersault. With her elbows on her knees, she pins me with a look that backs me up a couple of inches.

"Because! Because that day-to-day shit just ain't fun, okay? It's not fun and he didn't want to do it. And when it came time for the fun stuff he wanted to spend the little money he had on other things!"

"Then why did you put up with him? Really, you've been sleeping with him all these years?"

"Marva!"

"It's important, Ma. It makes a difference! Have you? Were you? That's what you're telling me, right?"

"Yes! Yes, that's what I'm telling you. He was good for some things but not for others. I took what I wanted and I did without the rest. But I didn't want you to make the same choice I did. I didn't want you to think that's all men were good for, that he was what a whole man looks like, so I didn't let you see what I was doing."

She's massaging her hands so hard I can almost feel it myself. I don't say anything and she continues. I can hear the pressure in her throat as her voice strains. Her eyes slide away from my stare.

"I've given him everything he wanted and *only* what he wanted, and now when I finally say what about me?… when I tell him that now I need his companionship, even more than I would have liked his help before, even more than I want his sex, what does he do? What's his reaction?! He has a hissy fit and gets himself killed! You see? Do you think that's the kind of man I wanted you to grow up around? To think that he was a good man? Yes, he had a good heart and a good mind, but he couldn't act on either of them!"

I put my glass down on the table very gently. It takes more control than usual. I stretch out on my back on the floor. From this vantage point I can see the dusty bottle of champagne on top of the kitchen cabinet. I got it at a wedding that Mommy took me to when I was seven. I don't even remember who's wedding, but I've kept the bottle. All these damn years.

I fall asleep. Or maybe fall asleep is a little generous. I pass the hell on out. When I wake up Mommy is gone, and I feel like a dried mushroom: raised in the dark, plucked from my roots, and baked 'til my essence leaked out.

Of course it could be the gin.

After a shower I start to feel a little better and I'm sitting on the couch trying to give myself a pedicure, but really I'm just playing with my toes like a child. I realize that as far as birds go, my father wasn't a good versatile bird, like a chicken, everybody's yardbird. He was more like a peacock. Good at what he did, apparently. But unable or unwilling to do anything else.

Lucky for me, my mother didn't raise no fool.

Cane and Jelly

I gon' tell you 'bout dis woman from down by me, 'bout how she had meddle in people business like she ain't had none a she own. She had like to keep people running through she mouth so much 'til people call she Telephone. Straight under she face. De children call she Miss Telephone.

She ain't feel no shame though. She say she only being who she is. And de worse part a de whole package? She like everybody conscience, which nobody ain't want.

So like Carnival time, she walk 'round wid she hand on she hip separating man from woman and woman from man. If she see two women yabba yabbing—at de beach, on de bus, or wheresoever—she stroll right up to dem and bust dem 'bout whatsoever she tink dey talking 'bout.

"Allyou shouldn't be talking 'bout how tight she dress is just 'cause allyou could see de size, shape, and hold of she batty. She look trampy, yes, but I gon' tell she so. I not like you, whisper, whisper behind people back." And Telephone go up to de lady getting on de bus wid she five bag a ting, she dress hike up trying to make de steps and "why you dress so short/tight, Donna Francis, Miss Rachel's child? You too old for after school clothes, you ain't in you yard, you in de street. Cover youself decent like—we don't wan see all you business."

Time come de people does grouch she back, but not too hard cause dey ain't had nothin much to scold she 'bout, just she mouth. Plus she ole.

She live 'pon de hill in a house she and she husband had build deyself. From blue bitch stone and shell and ting. T'is a sturdy house. But de outside a de wall, and de inside too, dey say, cover over wid all kind a hard ting from nature. We thought dat was she husband hand, but she da be out dere polishing de conch shells and dusting de stone so she musta be dey in dat too. He been dead for 'bout eighteen years. She children had done gon' Stateside long time. Dey had ask she come live wid dem, but she say no. So she dey dey, working and minding people.

But you know how you does get trip up in life? Whatsoever is you main ting, dat's de very ting dat you gon' get hit wid. And just so it happen to Telephone.

T'was a man from 'cross de water, St. Croix, same old as she, come live wid he daughter here on St. Thomas. He use to be a dockworker, forty-five years. He ain't never marry, but he had plenty wife and seven children. Of de five of he woman only one a cuss him, but all say he have de sweetest sugar cane dey ever taste. De children honor him though, cause he honor dem, so when Frienda build a small house for him in she side yard, he went go live with she.

Now dis man, Alphonso, Alfie, could do anyting wid board. If he walkin, he whittlin', but if he home, is a knocking and a pounding you gon' hear less he sleep. But first ting he want to do after he make heself situate in de new house is go to de market to see what kind a ting de people doing.

By dis time de market was only a place for old folks, tourists, and born bush people what wid everybody going Plaza Extra and K-mart. But anyting you could get a dem place you could get at de market. Even if you don't see it. And all de best ting you would never see, but you have to know how to ask.

Morning come, Alfie rambling down de road to town. He daughter, Frienda, stop on she way to work and offer him a ride in she car.

"Daddy, where you going so early? I thought you'd be sleeping, you retire and all."

"I got plenty time to sleep when I dead. No, I just going town to see what all a go on."

Frienda keeping pace wid she father crawl along de road. Traffic mighty slow down behind, but nobody ain't start to bawl yet, as dey woulda do it too.

"I gon' be living here now, so is best I make meself at home and see who is who and what is what. Who doing what I does do, and who doing what I might want to do."

"And who to do, too, eh?" Frienda say, laughing she deep throaty laugh.

Alfie stop. Stand up in de road. Frienda get scared, thinking even though she grown and married, she shouldn't be tryin talk grown people ting wid she father, who so grown more dan she.

Alfie wasn't studying 'bout takin she car ride before and after he hear dat he know he ain't. He tinking he gon' have to soap out she mouth, make she stop talking beef wid he. Or if is talk she wan talk, he could talk. But he ain't really know he daughter dat well again yet.

So he laugh.

And Frienda had understand every second of he silence, so she change de subject back, quick quick.

"Daddy, you want a ride?"

"No, I gon' just stroll, take me time. See who still rushing after buckra penny. Thank you."

And Frienda know she been put in she place. De cars behind starting to honk dey horns. Frienda say "OK, see you home tonight, unless you want meet me to my job, if you still in town come five o'clock. OK? Bye," and she zoom off.

Insteada de cars behind Frienda rushing to catch she, de inching by like dey ain't really going no place a'tall. All a dem inside twisting 'round to see who it 'tis had hold up de line so.

Alfie tink, humph. Good. Is good dey see me. I ain't going a place. And he "good morning" all a dem, many a who offer him a ride, too.

Dat was 'bout seven thirty. He reach de market after ten. He reach town thirsty bad, but he ain't want stop buy nothing to drink 'til he reach de market, being as he like to know where de money he spend gon' end up.

De market was de selfsame place dey had sell de slaves from in time gone. De old cement table dem, smoothe smoothe now. It had new tin roof though, and he sure when it rain it sound just like sweet steel pan.

Wid he callused hands in he pocket and he palm frond hat, which he sister make him three years ago, pull down low over he face, he circle de market two time, just looking. Finally he see somebody he recognize. Lemonhead. He look like de Backbreak family, all about de head and shoulders where Alfie could see. Das just how Alfie used to seeing him. Sitting down wid his hands between his knees. He play drums wid de scratch band. Drum so hard he get de ladies all lifting up dey dress whilst dey don't know what dey doing. Come off de dance floor and try tell one a dem dey was showing all kinda ting in de name of having room to maneuver and dey go tell you dey don't remember no such a ting and get from here with you forward self. Yeah, Lemonhead get de women all work up, he must know where and when anyting a go on.

So Alfie pick he way through de crowd a tourist milling 'round, dey watching him like he a relic for dey amusement. What allyou watching me so for? You lucky me ain't want go Kansas to coop you like poppy show. Humph.

Lemonhead see Alfie weaving towards him. He trying to place de face too. Man like dat should be easy to remember, he tinking. Alfe stand 'bout six feet four inches. Still a big man, wid a big belly too. Not too big, 'bout four, five months, carrying low. He still swing he body like he shifting weight from left to right and back again. Is a trial to watch him cause he arms and shoulders on one time and he hips and legs on another. And now, as he watching people on each side a him is like he head is de tail end of a donkey cart, turning de corner long after de donkey done gone.

"Hey, man. You is Lemonhead, right? From de band? I's Alfie, from St. Croix. I go almost every dance allyou play."

"Yeah? Alfie? Alfie is you name? I remember you. You take up a lotta room on de dance floor." Lemonhead reach out he hand to clasp Alfie own.

"So what you doing over here, man?"

"I come live wid me daughter. You might know she. Frienda Bishop. She work in de big jewelry store to de head a main street."

"Oh, so Frienda is your daughter, eh? I gon' remember dat." And he drop he eye back to he work, fastening a new skin on a old drum.

"Say, who I could get a cold drink from 'round here?"

"Go by my sister. She over dere in de big hat. Name Telephone."

Alfie knew just who he meant. Had noticed her right away. A sweet blackberry-skin woman wid a hat look like she in Easter parade. Lemonhead's sister, huh? What kind a name is Telephone? Is Telephone he say?

"She married?"

Lemonhead watch he so long 'til Alfie almost start to fidget. He cuss heself for letting a question like dat slip out so fast. He ain't even know dat he wanted to know. Just when he tink any more silence would make soup outta da bone Lemonhead finally speak.

"Been."

Been? Been? Been married for a long time? Or been married before but not now?

Alfie suck he teeth long and slow, seeing de ball and throwing it back. He turn off.

Lemonhead beat out a loud fast riff on he drum.

When Alfie reach Telephone's table he stand right behind she 'til she turn 'round and notice him.

"Good morning, daughter," he say, smiling wide.

She watch him up and down. Surprised he call she daughter. She ain't junior to him. She try turn she head to she table, but she eyes wander back on dey own.

"Good morning, daughter," he say again, exactly like de first time.

She bust out laughing. A loud guffaw dat she try lock down right away and end up choke coughing. Why dis man make she laugh, she ain't know. He just tickle she wid he old timey looking self and young daughter ting rolling off he tongue. Well, she couldn't ignore him no more, so she say "Good morning," pulling she lips tight together like it wasn't she just catch a joke.

"What you got to drink today?" Alfie ask.

"Same as I got every Tuesday," she mutter.

"Well, I'm new 'round here. So tell me, no? I could see dat's maubi and dat's lemonade, but what hold up in dem two big drums?"

"Ginger beer," she mumble, wondering why he cause she to act so, chewing she words like small piece a meat you can't self find in you mouth. So she catch up sheself and sing out, "Ginger beer. Ginger beer. Tuesday day I got strong ginger beer. I got weak ginger beer. I got cold maubi, yes, and coconut water, but 'tis very dear. I got sorrel and sea moss and Tuesday special, soursop. A quarter a taste, which is only a drop, a dollar a cup, which'll just hit de spot, or five for a bottle if—" she stopped.

Her voice so strong and clear Alfie feel he could see de notes in de air. He had like her song and was wanting to see how high she price would go.

"So, you know what you want?" she ask he, brazen, like he had do her something.

"Yeah, I'll take de maubi. Strong. A bottle. With a cup on de side. If you please."

She just watch he.

"And some ice, if you got any."

Well, dat set she off. "You tink you gon' put ice in my maubi? Nothing 'tall go so. Get from 'round me and go by de drugstore for a soda."

"You don't want make me a sale?" Alfie still smiling, ain't take offense. He know he getting to her but he ain't' know why, 'less is his charm and good looks, which case it good. He ain't gon' have to work hard atall.

"Me ain't need you money. You ain't see de crush a people I just serve? And is early. I got plenty left."

"And you gon' deny me? I thirsty, you know? Walk all de way from hillside. You brother tell me you had good ting." He shut off he smile like a gust a wind blow de window shut. Closed he eye dem slowly, letting he eye holes roam down de length a she body, slowly enough for she to notice.

Well, Telephone shocked, you hear? She don't used to making mistake 'bout people, but it seem a ridiculous ting going on here dis morning. He flirting wid she!

And worse yet? She liking it.

Alfie let he hand dem squirm 'round in he pocket. De only movement between dem. Dis maubi must be really sweet under de tart, he tink.

Telephone bring out a bottle a maubi. A old scotch bottle wid de J & B label still intact. She peel off a paper cup and set it beside de bottle. He want a bag? she tink. No, he gon' drink it now. But he gon' drink de whole bottle one time? No. Give he a bag. Plus you ain't want him in de street with a scotch bottle, right? What? I must care? Is what do me anyway? She bust out laughing again, amazed at she own confusion. He mubbe some kinda a jumbie to get she going on so.

Alfie figured de "been" Lemonhead spoke of been gone long time, and Telephone, or whatsoever she name, don't used to laughing.

"So you gon' give me a bag?"

"Is you who want a cup. I figure you gone drink it down right here." She slide de bottle and cup nearer to him, but he have to come closer to reach it. She hold she breath.

No one ain't move.

Lemonhead's drumming change de tempo of de moment, and Telephone puff out, "So what you gon' do?" just as Alfie ask, "So how much you want?"

Next ting you know Telephone ain't Telephone no more. Now she is Agatha. Not Agatha, mind you, but Ahh-GAA-ta, wid a whole lotta breathy rolling around in de throat and a sharp sweet end to it like guavaberry wine. De people at church say, "you see Ahh-GAA-ta come to church without no hat? Humph." De neighbors say "you see how Ahh-GAA-ta friend dere to load up de car at foreday morning? Where he come from?" De follow band posse say, "you see how she rolling she bumsy like she been doing it all de time? What? She been practicing in she bedroom? She almost as good as Marva!"

Day come, day go. Alfie sit at de market, halfway between Lemonhead and Agatha, whittlin' and carving. He make little stands for she bottles with hinges so dey could tip over to pour out dollar cups. He make holds for de five gallon drums, so dey don't roll around in de car. He was gon' make a tool box for Lemonhead but dat was before dey had words.

Lemonhead had watch him wid cut eye 'til Alfie had to ask him what do he? When he get de understanding he was plenty mad. If Alfie had been strutting behind de young chickens wid new feathers den Lemonhead woulda just laugh and keep all he man secrets, but cause Alfie want he mind, he heart, and he wine all in one big full-grown woman, is trouble. Like he breaking de man rules, buttering and beefing what ain't supposed to have no taste no more.

And Telephone. Agatha. She drop right down from an authority to an example. Mothers say to prideful children "watch youself now, mind you don't turn out like Miss Ahh-GAA-ta. All who rise must fall."

You tink Telephone care atall? Now she go 'bout she bidness wid such a smile on she face dat people know she back teeth by name. Is so she tell dem, "I work hard all me life, as a wife, and a mother, in de shops and de hotels, in de church, for me friends. After Henry dead, is anybody see me? Is anybody say is I could make she smile? No. Allyou man tink is alright to ignore me once I ain't young. Well, is time make sweet wine, you hear?"

De people ain't tired talk 'bout how she and Alfie was playing catch in de yard, throwing ball back and forth like dey was children. 'Bout how dey take up long stick and was practicing wid de majorettes from across de street. De little girls dem giggling to see two old people trying to twirl baton. Dey go movies every week, no matter what showing. Dey go fishing, and a fisherman say he see dem skinny dipping at Mandahl Bay. Dey even say dey gon' be single entry in de parade this year. Cane Juice and Coconut Jelly.

Neida one a dem got a bit a shame.

Mrs. Aswald's Time

Lisa works. Lisa has a job as a secretary and earns fourteen thousand dollars a year. Lisa has two daughters who she says are the joy of her life.

And she means it. They are Lisa's joy in that in between the hours of homework and the bickering and the fact that one can't stand having her hair combed and the other doesn't like water to touch her skin and neither of them eagerly eats anything that isn't advertised during Saturday morning cartoons, there are incidences that bring a smile to her heart. No one else touches it. The girl's father had ceased to have access to it. Her parents and two brothers are people she knows it would be better not to associate with. Her life seems endless in that she is twenty-three and in good health. Sometimes she wishes she could be like some of the old folks whose charts she maintains at the nursing home. Like Mrs. Aswald and her best friend Ellie Minty. Both over eighty-five and pulling each other through the days as if they were on a cruise.

But admiration is one of the lesser emotions. It certainly isn't enough to motivate Lisa. She knows she should do something. She knows that women have changed their lives from drab and depressing to exciting, satisfying, or at least commendable. College is out of the question. She couldn't afford a babysitter even if she could pay the tuition, and besides, she knows what happens to children left in the care of strangers. No, college is no good. But a correspondence course, at least, or a small business. An at-home business. Something. Anything. Soon.

"You look like a nice Christian girl. Have you met my son?"

"I don't go to church and I have two illegitimate daughters, Mrs. Aswald."

"Now, don't you try to shock me, young lady. I've been watching you since the day you got here, and I know who you are. Now, I asked you a question and you answer me with respect."

Lisa turned to really look at Mrs. Aswald for the first time in a few days. According to her chart Mrs. Aswald could go any day now. She had her bad days when she saw, or felt, people standing over her shoulder or when she commanded you to do the impossible, like bring the tree outside her window inside so she could repot it. Or call her husband, James (775-2797) who'd been dead for eleven years, to come and get her because she was ready to go now, thank you very much. But today, today as Lisa looked into Mrs. Aswald's eyes, she saw that today was a good day.

"No, I don't think I've met your son, Mrs. Aswald," Lisa said, stirring the coffee she'd come in to the activities room to get.

"Well, you will. And marry him too. He's coming here today. What's your extension? He needs someone to live for and you need someone to love. Other than the two, umm, but you leave at five, don't you? Ordinarily, I mean."

Mrs. Aswald rolled her wheelchair to the door as Lisa eased away, hemming her in, leaving just enough space between Lisa's small frame and the wall for Lisa to high step over the wheels and get away.

At five minutes to five Lisa's phone rang, and she knew she wouldn't be leaving this purgatory in five minutes after all. Ellie Minty was in cardiac arrest, and even though the staff knew that there was a Do Not Resuscitate order on file for her, Mrs. Aswald refused to believe it. Refused to believe that her friend, one of the most life-grabbing people she'd ever known, had agreed to such a preposterous thing. Imagine, giving in to the ghost when there was still time to see if Mr. Brandson in 3B could get it up again, or if Mary Shirley's nephew would smuggle in another bottle of rum before Bingo Night? The staff must be mistaken, she insisted.

"Mixed up. Mad. Mad as the death watch witches you are! It was forged! It's a fake! You don't know what you're doing. I'll wake her up!"

Mrs. Aswald wielded her wheelchair like a chariot and got in everyone's way until she was finally chased back to the activities room.

For Lisa five to five had come too late. She'd had to pull Ellie Minty's file and call the doctor on duty and the hospital and the relatives and her daughters after school program, all through blurry eyes and a bubbling mass of sadness in her throat.

Mrs. Aswald wheeled herself to the after-hours entrance at precisely five twenty-five. Jacob arrived at five twenty-seven. She'd never kept such good track of time before coming to Sunny Valley, but now, since coming here, time was a companion she liked to keep close. If dinner was not served at six thirty, or her pain killer, the pink one, did not arrive every four hours, she knew. The digital watch Jacob had given her helped her mark the time in a way she'd never needed before. And at five twenty-seven the doors at both end of the long hallway opened. From the buildings' interior with desperation. From the outside with resignation.

Adrenalin ignited Mrs. Aswald's brain, and she was not sure who to greet first. This is important, she told herself, don't mess up.

"Hi, Mama. How're you doing today?"

"Jacob, my watch is working just fine and I just want you to know, you know, I'm trying to tell you about time, no about Ellie Minty, she doesn't have any more you know, not a watch, a time, not anymore and she'd tell you, if she were here, the same thing. You see this girl? Sneaking up in back of me? That one? You marry her, you hear? Don't look at me like that. I know what time it is. Now, I'ma introduce you, hear?"

"Mrs. Aswald, I really have to go now, may I get by please?"

Lisa had taken thirty-five small and silent steps to the halfway point of the long hallway, and her voice quavered as for the second time that day she tried to edge past Mrs. Aswald's wheelchair.

"No, not yet," Mrs. Aswald shouted. "You don't have a minute?" She swung her chair into Lisa's knee, "Here, I'll give you some of mine," she said, scratching at her wrist to get her watch off.

Lisa's skirt, the only one she liked, got caught on the brake lever and she heard the sounds of threads snapping as she slowly pulled toward her escape. Toward the door, the bus stop, her only joy.

Jacob tried to smile at Lisa, but his eyes would not meet hers, and he ended up smirking at her skirt, hoping she would understand the ramblings of an old woman.

"Let me help you with that," he said, squatting down to detangle fabric from machine.

Lisa stood still while Jacob worked dangerously close to her left knee. Mrs. Aswald got her watch off and shook it at Lisa.

"There, Lisa, time. Now, Jacob, like I said, this is someone very important in your life. Me and James want you to love her and treat her right, you hear? She got two, umm, two umm, illuminated children and they want to glow too. And Lisa, that's Lisa right there, Ellie Minty just said she got too much time left to be lonely, and she's a good girl. Jacob? Jacob, are you listening to me? What're you fiddling with down there? Stand up straight!"

"Good night, Mrs. Aswald," Lisa said, "I'll see you tomorrow."

"Yes, that's right, tomorrow..."

Jacob had straightened up and was trying to turn the wheelchair around in the narrow corridor.

"And thank you, Jacob, for freeing my skirt."

"Yes, Lisa, that's right, tomorrow," Mrs. Aswald said, "what time?"

The hallway dance was over, with both Jacob and Lisa poised to move off in opposite directions. Mrs. Aswald looked over her right shoulder, trying to dislodge Jacob's hand from the handles and push him aside.

"Eight o'clock? Right?" she called, "You'll be here at eight, right? Lisa? But I won't see you until ten eighteen, right? When you come to get coffee? Am I right? Now Jacob," she looked up at him, tilting her head upwards, still trying to get his hand off the back handles, "you walk Lisa to her car, hear? And ask her to marry you. No, not yet. First ask her about herself, hear? And her two irrigation sisters, umm, you know how to do it. Go on now. Shoo! I'll see you later, when you get back. Look for me in my room. I have to get ready, James and I are going dancing, you know. After dinner, at six thirty, at eight."

Responding in Kind

"Dat girl ain't got no sense atall! I don't care how upset she is, she got no business leaving me beggin' at no graveyard. Took me damn car. My car! I should bust she one good cuff upside she head. She too hardened. Wouldn't listen to me. Never listened to me. Well, who don't hear must feel. The only thing she use she ears for is to hold up them oversize earrings. I tried to warn her. I knew that damn boy was no damn good, that one that started this whole mess, don't care who his people is. She listen to me? No, I tell you! She start smellin' her pee, think she grown, and now here we is buryin' a baby. Ain't that bad enough? Bad enough, I tell you. Me ain' never bury one a me own babies, and here one a my babies buryin' a child. That's bad enough. But is that enough?! Enough for one damn day? No, she gotta go and steal me damn car!"

"Mommy, I wouldn't call it stealing, exactly."

"No. You wouldn't, would you?" Lorraine cut her eye at her only son, Gerald. He looked so much like her memories of his father, with his face so narrow and dark that his features seemed concentrated, that it often confused her sense of time.

"Just be cool, Mommy. Nobody's having a good day."

She thought about throwing the dish of macaroni and cheese at him, but didn't. Only because it was Mrs.

Milligan's dish. The one she bought from the stumpy guy who came by selling stuff out of the trunk of his car. She remembered Mrs. Milligan inspecting the two-quart baking dish as if it were fine crystal. And then deciding to buy it because it was made in Taiwan and her son had been there during his travels with the army, which was the only practical way he could think of for escaping the Virgin Islands and his mother.

The kitchen door swung open and banged against the refrigerator. "Mommy! People comin! Wha to do wid dem?"

"What you think you s'posed to do with them? Pitch them over the railing? Shit!"

Ameka, unscathed, looked to Gerald.

"Put them to sit down in the living room. If they brought any food, you bring it in here. And ask them if they want something to drink. Anything else, Mommy?"

Lorraine ignored them both as she shoved a chair against the fridge and climbed up to get the bottles of liquor she kept in the upper cabinets.

Ameka skated back down the length of the hallway in new patent leather shoes.

"And where dat odda sorry ass was, anyhow? If he'da been dere she wouldn'ta even tink ta drive she ownself home from no damn funeral in de first place!" She backed off the chair with her last bottle of Johnnie Walker Red held by the neck.

"What you bringing him up for? He ain't been on the scene since she told him she was pregnant. You want me to get some glasses or you gon' use paper cups?"

"You just reach Rhonda's tray down here, and I'll do the rest." She paused, then added loudly, hoping he heard a command instead of a plea, "I want you to go get your sister."

Gerald brought down the brass tray one of his girl-friends had stolen the night of their Mexican restaurant dinner date and given to his mother for Christmas. He thought about bringing down the other tray too, the one from McDonald's, but decided against it.

"Mommy, why you don't let Derri rest, no?"

"Look boy, just shut up and go do wha Ah tol you! Ah don' need you to be second-guessing me today, you hear?! You don't know shit! Go get her I said!"

"No." Gerald cracked the ice trays on the chipped, spotlessly clean, yellow laminated countertop.

"None a you worth a hill a beans. Alla you just a big pain in my barna, all 'cept Pookie, she de only one a you got de least little bit a sense. Gatha up dem glasses and put dem on de tray, no? What you standing 'round for? Dere's reasons dere's so much work for a family to do after a buryin', you know."

"No, Mommy, leave her alone."

"And see if she got my bottle of Cruzan Gold in dere with she. De liddle tief."

Gerald balanced the tray of glasses in one hand and the bowl of ice in the other. He kicked open the kitchen door, hoping Ameka wasn't on the other side with a platter full of chicken or something. "I ain't going, Mommy."

Lorraine sighed. It had been a long time since she'd been able to tell Gerald what to do.

She passed Ameka in the hall carrying a pan of potato stuffing with Pookie behind her struggling with a pot of rice and beans.

"Who all dere?" she asked, regretting for the zillionth time that she'd have to go through the living room to get to the bedrooms.

"A bunch a people. Miss Potter and Miss Soto and dat funny lookin' lady wha' always smell so stink, and Leon and Ray—"

But Lorraine was already there. She put on a grief-stricken dazed expression and weaved through the crowd unstopped.

"Now Derecia, I know how you feel," Lorraine began as soon as she closed the door behind her, the room that housed the crib, the crib the baby barely slept in, so up in arms was he, "but you gotta get up."

Derecia lay on her back on the twin bed closest to the door. The bottle of rum dangled from one hand while Jakiel's crib sheet was pressed into service as part blanket and part tissue by the other.

"How you gon' know how I feel?" Derecia tried to root herself deeper into the cushiness of the soft mattress.

At least she can still talk, thought Lorraine.

"Because everybody knows pain. Everybody knows sorrow. Dat's why all dese people here today. Trying to… trying to…say dey're sorry too. Trying to share de load of grief wid you. Come on, get up and show some respect for de consideration dey're showing you."

"Dat's bullshit, Mommy. Dey here for de party. For de food and some a dis rum. Buh, dat's whey dey lose out." Derecia tipped the bottle to her lips, like an experienced drunk, Lorraine thought, "becharse…because Ah ain't sharing. And Ah ain't goin' out dere neida."

"You gotta get up. I need you to help me. Derri, dere's food to set out and glasses to fill, and yes, I tell you, condolences to accept. Dey can't give you your son back, but you gon' have to take what dey can give. Get up, baby."

"Well, if dey can' gea me wha Ah wan', wha Ah mus do wid dem? Ah don' need look at dere ugly faces jus to hear dem say wha dey s'pose to say, is all poppyshow, anyhow."

She shifted her gaze to the ceiling. "No, I ain' goin' out dey. Ah wish everybody jus' drop dead. Jus' drop dead…lak…like Jakiel. Jus' wake up dead."

Lorraine looked at her eighteen-year-old daughter, the most confused of her four children. Half the tears she'd cried in the last five days had been for Derecia. Derecia, with her smile as powerful as high noon thundershowers and her far flung ambitions, now forgotten. Derecia, who was so smart in so many ways and so astonishingly dumb in others. The girl really didn't seem to know what had happened to her life during the past year and a half. And she didn't have a clue as to how to go on either, how to piece together the semblance of a functional woman from the shattered leftovers of a child.

"You get up and go out in de living room right now, 'fore I give you wha' Polly gea' de drum!" Lorraine found herself yanking open the closet door, almost as if her body moved instinctively, "Ah ain' axin' you! Ah tellin' you! Do it now, else Ah whip you ass and den you *still* goin' out."

She wrestled a wide red plastic belt off a hanger as Derecia watched, ready to spring to the other side of the bed, not sure how far her mother would really go.

Lorraine started showering the air with blows as soon as she had a good grip on the belt. The third swing caught Derecia on the toes. She curled up and rolled over, the open bottle of rum going with her, sloshing onto her clothes and soaking the bed.

"Get up, you fool! Look what you doin! You gon' have de place stinkin' like de drunk you tryna play! Stop dis silliness and act like you got good sense!"

Derecia jumped up on the middle of the bed. Her black crepe dress hiked up around firm hips and still soft belly. She waved the bottle widely in front of her and jumped from bed to bed.

"Stop! Mommy, stop! Ah warnin' you! Somebody gon' gea hurt! Stop!"

"You?! You warnin' me?! Well, wha' kinda day dis is, no? Ah gon' tear your butt up, and de more mess you make in dis room, de worse it gon' be!"

The door opened and faces of all ages and degrees of concern appeared. Mrs. Milligan's lilac bulk took up most of the doorway, but she was framed by Gerald, whose flared nostrils and bitten lips signaled that he was ready to mash Mrs. Milligan through the plasterboard wall if he had to, and Ameka, who burst out with the high pitched giggle she was calling a laugh this week, and Pookie, who peeked through fingers covered in barbeque sauce, and Leon, who looked bewildered, not sure if he had the right to yell, or who to yell at.

"Wha goin' on in heh?" Mrs. Milligan's melodic bass, which always seemed to come from her massive breasts, penetrated the other ruckus easily, even though she was not the loudest.

"Mommy!"

Lorraine noticed that her title exploded from Gerald with the tone of command he used on his so-called friends.

"Derri getting beat! Derri getting beat!" Ameka chanted.

"Ah thought you say we s'posed ta be nice ta Derri today," Pookie said.

"Get out!" shouted Lorraine. "Get out, alla you!"

Derecia threw her legs out from under her and bounced butt first on the bed, capping the bottle of rum with her thumb.

Mrs. Milligan sidestepped the others and closed the door in their faces.

"Millie, you too. I'm handlin' her."

"Ah ain' no horse," mumbled Derecia.

"You doin' a piss poor job of it, Lorraine. Now, Derecia, what all dis roogadoo about?"

"Eh-Eh, Miss Millie." Derecia turned the bottle of Cruzan up to her mouth and drank while Mrs. Milligan clasped her hands under her ballooning stomach and waited. Lorraine collapsed on the nearest bed.

"Ah can' be bodda, boddared wid ya nosy self today. Ah tired."

Lorraine flicked the belt uselessly in Derecia's direction.

Mrs. Milligan sucked in more air than Derecia thought possible. They stared at each other until Derecia crossed her ankles and began caressing her toes with her other foot.

"Mommy, Ah tink you broke me toe, you know."

"I been watchin' you and lovin' you since from de time you and you Mommy first moved in heh 'cross de hall from me when you was no mor'n a pea in pod. I seen wha' you been through and wha you facin' now, and Ah standing heh waitin' for you ta tell me wha' alla dis yellin and carryin' on is 'bout."

Derecia tried hard to tell the old lady to mind her own business, but the words burst like bubbles before they reached her tongue. She remembered the day they moved into this apartment. She hadn't liked anything about the place. The buildings towering over her, with windows like rotten teeth, vicious-looking dogs roaming the parking lot, the bones of abandoned cars. The steps to their third floor new home were hard for her four-year-old legs to manage, and when she looked between the porch railings she saw a rusted toaster, half a bike, forgotten laundry, and a rainbow of empty bottles. After forty eleven hundred trips up and down the stairs Miss Millie offered her some limeade in a pretty glass. A glass glass with colors that came and went like magic. When she'd finished drinking Miss Millie told her to "keep workin' chile, we gon' talk togedda soon."

"I'm tryna get de little heifer to come out and act decent," said Lorraine.

They may as well have been alone, Mrs. Milligan and Derecia.

Lorraine said nothing more. Her raspy breathing calmed slowly, noticeably.

Derecia's eyes started to glisten. "Ahdonwansee-nobody."

"You 'shamed, chile? You got nothin' ta be shamed fo'. We all know you was takin' good care of Jakiel. Can' nobody s'plain de Lord's way. Can' nobody s'plain crib death neida. But we all know you was a good Mudda and he was a sweet liddle boy. T'ain your fault, girl. We know dat. An we gon' miss him too. We heh to tell you dat."

"Das, das, dat ain'—"

"Yes, t'is. But wha you ain' say is deh's mo'. You tink people judgin' you. Because you took up wid dat high falutin', wicked boy everybody buh you could see was evil, an' he went an make you look like a fool, jus' wha' any bad man woulda do wid you actin like such a fool. An' den cause you next go an get youself in de family way by any ol' wormy apple wha' fall off de tree. An' den you went an' quit school even doh dey was gon' lea' you stay and try make something a youself, an' now you heh widout chit nor chile and you tink we judgin' you." Mrs. Milligan took another deep breath, "an' you right."

Lorraine's head snapped up, "I thought you was gon' try an make her feel better," she said.

"Of course we judgin' you. So wha? You hear me? So what? You ain' spread off dere judging de rest a we? You calling me nosy. So wha' now? You 'speck me ta run go hide from you? Not ta share me coconut candy wid you no more? Not to ask you to come take me curtains down when dey need to wash? No. Don' run from people, chile. Come out in de living room. We mournin' Jakiel, we need to be togedda."

"Shit, Millie, you's a two hundred fifty pound waste a time," said Lorraine.

Mrs. Milligan didn't bother to respond. She'd known Lorraine when she was still drowning the death of Gerald's father in other men's tears. Had seen her go from needful of arms that held to distrustful of arms that trapped, burdened, and beat. Thank God for Leon, though, he was starting to help. Lorraine she'd deal with later.

"Bring you bottle wid you, if you have ta. Ah gon' wait right heh."

Derecia didn't want to look up. Didn't want to see Miss Millie's stonelike face. She couldn't escape it though, her image was there in her dead babies' crib sheet. Pastel sheep, flowers and fish formed the pattern between Miss

Millie's broad brown forehead and jaw. Fishy eyes of still bright reddish brown, sheepish nose and flower teeth. Miss Millie had out-waited her before.

She got up, eyes on the ever swaying worn linoleum tiles. She stumbled once and heard Miss Millie's rumbling "das all right, chile," as she followed Miss Millie's leather soled flats down the hall. You could tell Miss Millie had good legs when she was young she thought.

Pookie emerged from her hiding place in the hallway between the chest of drawers that was used as a linen closet and the stack of milk crates that held up the ceiling tiles with books and records. Derecia switched the Cruzan Rum and crib sheet to the other hand as Pookie took firm hold of her knee.

"Jakiel don' live heh no mo'," Pookie whispered.

Derecia drew her little sister closer, then struggled to lift her up. They crashed against the walls on their way to the only vacant space on the couch.

Author Biography

I reach! On St. Thomas, Virgin Islands "I reach" is one way of saying that you have arrived, you're at the door. So yes, I reach. I was born, but, even my mother said that I acted like I wasn't from around here. Pretty as the earth is, fascinating as people are, I've always had the feeling that this is not my home, and so I write.

When I was young, an "other mother" of mine gave me a journal titled "How Can I Know What I Think Until I See What I Say?" and that, for me, is one of the great fringe benefits of writing.

Happily ensconced now in Harlem, New York, I'm a Virgin Islander through the Head of Main Street Bryans and the St. Johnian McKetneys, and I think writing is how we explain the unexplainable, sometimes to our liking.

Presently I'm working on a speculative fiction novel about a saint who reluctantly finds herself in the body of a Black woman in New York City about 50 years from now.